Casino Heat (Reunited Series)

Sharon C. Cooper

Amaris Publishing LLC

Casino Heat

ISBN: 978-1-946172-34-1

Acknowledgments

Huge shout out to Women of Faith book club! I appreciate you ladies!

Prologue

Moonlight shone through the open blinds, casting just enough illumination over his customer's face for Frankie to witness panic in the man's eyes. That's exactly what he wanted. It was three o'clock in the morning, the perfect time to inflict pain and instill the fear of God into a person who refused to pay up. Ironically enough, the man was standing in front of the bed, trembling, while wearing boxer shorts with dollar bills printed on them.

"Do you know what I do to people who owe me money? I make an example of them," Frankie explained.

He and Keith, one of his enforcers, had snuck into the punk's apartment and yanked him out of bed. By the time they were done with him, the guy wouldn't sleep again until he paid what he owed.

Well, he wouldn't sleep comfortably.

"Come on, Frankie, I'm gonna pay." Lester's gaze bounced nervously between Frankie and Keith, who was standing a few feet away with a baseball bat in his hands. "Don't I always pay?

I promise I'll get your money to you tomorrow. Just one more day. That's all I need."

Frankie was still pacing but stopped in front of the loser, literally. He'd been dealing with Lester for years, but lately the guy had been on a losing streak. And as a bookie, Frankie didn't take too kindly to people who found every excuse not to pay their debt. But that wasn't the worst of it.

"You pulled a knife on me," Frankie said, shoving the guy backward. Lester swayed, almost falling onto the bed but righted himself.

"Frankie," Lester whined. "You woke me out of a deep sleep. I thought you were a burglar. I freaked out. I meant no disrespect. I just...I just reacted."

"Yeah? Well, this is me reacting. "

Frankie popped Lester with a right hook to his jaw, sending the guy flying backward onto the bed. Ignoring how his skinny ass cried out in pain, Frankie grabbed him by the ear and forced him into a standing position.

"As I was saying, I want my money. *Now!*" he roared.

Lester jumped, then stumbled over to the nightstand, tripping over his gym shoes, and grabbed the cash off the top. "I—I only have two hundred. Give me one more day, and I promise I'll have the rest."

Frankie snatched the crumpled bills and counted them. As he stuffed the money into the front pocket of his jeans, he jerked his head toward Keith.

"Sure, you can have another day, but this is what happens to people who don't pay me on time."

Keith stepped forward and, with lightning speed, swung the bat, catching the left side of Lester's knee as if he was trying to hit a baseball out of the park. The young punk crumbled to the floor, howling like a wounded bear.

If his neighbors were asleep, they were awake now.

Frankie headed to the door but stopped and glanced over his shoulder. "We'll be back tomorrow for the rest, and if your ass doesn't have it, you'll never walk again. Have a good night."

Chapter One

"He's dead," Viviana Connelly murmured into the quietness of the huge, all-white family room. "He's dead...and I'm free."

She glanced down at the silver-framed photo of her and Thomas in her hand. Her husband was dead, and so many emotions swirled inside her, warring with each other. But not one of those emotions included sadness.

Regret, maybe—but definitely not sadness.

Viviana's eyes zoomed in on her unsmiling face in the picture.

She rarely smiled when they were together. There'd been nothing to smile about. Hell, it had taken everything within her to drum up enough energy to even stand next to the bastard.

Seven years. Seven excruciating years of living with a man who forced her away from a life of love and happiness. In its place—he had blackmailed her into a loveless marriage.

Viviana gritted her teeth and gripped the photo tighter. She wanted to hurl the picture through the floor-to-ceiling windows and scream, *Thank you, God, he's dead!*

But she refrained.

Part of her was afraid that someone was playing a cruel joke, making her believe that she was finally free. Making her believe that she no longer had to live under the same roof with a man she never loved. Making her believe that she no longer had to put up with the man who had crushed her joy and destroyed her life.

But it was true. She had seen his body. She knew he was dead.

"I'm free. I'm finally free," she repeated.

She sighed loudly and slowly turned, taking in her surroundings as if seeing everything for the first time. White furniture, marbled floors, and a hideous mural of her late husband on the largest wall in the house was what she saw. The painting was the only splash of color in the room and looking at it made her want to spit on it...spit on *him*.

His pretentious billionaire ass had been so full of himself, thinking that he hung the sun and the moon. What made it worse was that people had treated him as such. Viviana never thought she could hate another human being as much as she'd hated him.

Her heart rate amped with thoughts of all that she'd endured over the years, but her horrible life hadn't been all Thomas's fault. No, she owned some of the blame. Actually, most of it. Helping, supporting, and trusting the wrong people had finally been her downfall, and Thomas, the ruthless businessman, had cashed in. She'd left herself vulnerable one too many times and doing so had practically squeezed the life from her.

Never again.

As of that moment, she was taking charge and planned to live the life she'd dreamed of having. She was never letting another person manipulate her into doing anything she didn't want to do, no matter what. It had been a hard lesson to learn, but thanks to Thomas, it had finally sunk in.

He's dead.

Viviana shook her head, still trying to process what that really meant. There'd been so many times that she'd wanted to leave him and suffer whatever consequences, but she hadn't. She stuck it through and had planned on staying for another three years, which would've been ten total.

But now...

"I'm free."

"Mrs. Reagan?"

Viviana startled and turned to find the housekeeper, Sara, standing in the wide opening into the family room. Her salt-and-pepper hair was pulled back into a severe bun at her nape, giving a clear view of her round, tanned face and the concern in her eyes.

"Yes, Sara?" Viviana said, and set the framed photo face down on the white marbled sofa table.

"Is there anything you need or anything I can get you?" Sara asked. She was visibly nervous as she ran the palms of her hands over her rounded hips and down the sides of her conservative black dress.

Viviana hated that they had a full staff for the house, and Thomas had insisted that they wear a uniform. The simple outfit was accented with white trim around the collar on the bottom of the short sleeves.

The woman was probably nervous for herself, as well as the staff. Sara was not only Viviana's personal attendant, but she oversaw all of housekeeping; basically, anything that had to do with the interior of the home.

Viviana was going to miss the woman who'd been nothing but kind to her from the moment they'd met.

"Thank you, Sara, I don't need anything. But just so that

you know, my name is Viviana Connelly. Feel free to call me Viviana—and please don't ever call me Mrs. Reagan again. That person doesn't exist." *She never did.*

Surprise showed on Sara's face, and she bowed slightly. "Yes, ma'am. If you need anything, I'll be—"

"You and the staff take the rest of the day off," Viviana blurted.

Sara frowned. "Ma'am? But what will you eat? Who will clean?"

Instead of responding to her questions, Viviana said, "As a matter of fact, take the next three days off until I decide next steps. Consider it a much-deserved paid time off."

Worry marred the older woman's tanned face. No doubt she was concerned about the future of her job.

She was right to be concerned. There was no way Viviana was staying in that home any longer than she had to. She hated the place almost as much as she'd hated Thomas.

"Give me a few days to figure things out, Sara, and I'll be in touch. Okay?"

"Yes, ma'am," Sara said. "Please don't hesitate to call me if you need me to return sooner. I'll be leaving shortly."

"Thanks, Sara."

After the woman walked away, Viviana headed up the spiral staircase to the bedroom she'd shared with Thomas. The six-bedroom, eight-bathroom mansion was located in MacDonald Highlands, an exclusive neighborhood in Henderson, Nevada.

The home had once been featured in *Architectural Digest*, but the only spaces in the house that Viviana liked were her closet that was as large as a bedroom, and the sitting room adjacent to the master bedroom. Both places offered a retreat away from Thomas.

Viviana pushed open the double doors to the master bedroom and made a beeline to the bathroom. After taking the fastest shower in history, she dressed carefully, opting for a hot pink linen suit that belted around the waist of the jacket. It was lightweight enough for summer in Vegas, but warm enough for air-conditioned buildings. She'd pair the outfit with matching block heel mules, but for now, she stuck her feet into her favorite pair of Crocs.

Now came the real work—packing her belongings. She planned to take everything she wanted because she had no intentions of returning to the house once she was gone.

She grabbed several large suitcases from the corner of the closet and started filling them. She wasn't sure how long she'd been hard at work when she heard someone call out to her in the distance.

"Viviana?"

Viviana moved out of the closet at the sound of her best friend's voice.

"I'm upstairs," she called out.

A few minutes later, Dannette Bell bonded into the room. "Where are you?"

"In the closet packing some of my things."

Viviana glanced up when Dannette appeared in the doorway. Her dreadlocks were pulled up on top of her head with a few braids framing her pretty face. She and Dannette were close in height at around five feet six, but her friend was a little thicker, with an hourglass figure that made grown men drool.

She always looked model-ready and today was no different. Wearing a navy-blue and white stripe sleeveless jumpsuit, the outfit glided over her curves and dipped in to show off her small waist. She had paired the garment with blue pumps that would no doubt be kicked off the moment she returned to her desk.

Dannette stepped into the space and hugged her. Viviana returned the hug, grateful that she was there. They had met shortly after Viviana had moved to Las Vegas from LA, and had bonded immediately. If it weren't for their friendship, Viviana didn't know what she would've done the last few years, especially since she didn't have siblings. Her only living relative, as far as she knew, was her mother, who she hadn't seen or heard from in years, which was for the best. Dannette had filled that family void and was closer than a sister.

They had become even closer, especially after Dannette lost her job five years ago. Viviana had hired her to be her executive assistant. It was one of the best decisions she'd ever made. Her friend had become so much more than that when it came to helping run TGR Grand Hotel and Casino, one of the largest casinos on the Las Vegas Strip.

"All things considered, you look amazing," Dannette said, waving a hand up and down, indicating Viviana.

Viviana glanced at the full-length mirror on the wall to her right and took in her appearance. Her curly pixie cut with a long bang swept over her right eye complemented her face, and the bright color of her outfit seemed to make her mocha skin tone glow.

She definitely didn't look like a woman who had just lost her husband. Viviana didn't feel like one either.

Though she was scared to death of things to come as it related to Thomas and dealing with his estate, she appeared strong and capable. That was something she'd always aimed for since overseeing the operations at the casino. It didn't matter that Thomas had broken her spirit in some ways—no one would ever know that once she stepped into her office. Her insides might shiver like a bowl of Jell-O, but her outer appearance reflected a badass businesswoman.

"Thanks," she finally said to her friend. "This outfit always makes me feel powerful."

Dannette nodded and grinned. "Good choice. Now let's hurry." She started pulling a few designer purses and shoes off the shelves of the custom closet and set them on the long dressing table. "So far there's no media outside, but it's only a matter of time. There were a couple of calls at the office before I left. People wanting to know if it was true that Thomas Reagan had passed away."

"What did you tell them?" Viviana asked as she unzipped another suitcase. As fast as she was moving, she felt as if she was getting ready to run away from home. Technically, that's exactly what she was doing. She had no intentions of staying in Thomas's house any longer than necessary.

"I played dumb. I told them I had no idea what they were talking about, but we should probably get ahead of this situation. Maybe you can pick a reporter to talk to before the media hears about Thomas's heart attack."

"I think it's safe to assume they already know," Viviana said on a sigh.

Thomas had died two hours ago. She'd barely had time to process that she was a widow. The last thing she wanted to do was talk to anyone, but she'd have to eventually make some phone calls. She also needed to get to the office and meet with the staff.

As the director of operations at TGR Grand, she would prefer the staff hear the news from her. But with the ever-present media and social media, it was safe to say that the news had already started spreading. Soon her cell phone would be ringing like crazy from her management team, wondering what was going on and if what they were hearing was true.

Thomas was an important figure in the community, and his casino and hotel was one of the largest and most popular on the

Strip—thanks to her hard work. Everyone would have questions and wonder about the future of the organization.

Too bad she wouldn't have many answers, at least not until she talked to Walter Underwood, Thomas's attorney. The man knew far more about Thomas and his estate than she did.

Viviana's heart beat a little faster, and suddenly feeling overwhelmed, she leaned forward with her hands on her thighs.

Just breathe. Just slow down and breathe, she told herself over and over again.

Eventually, she sucked in several deep breaths and released them slowly before Dannette placed her hand on her back.

"Maybe you should sit down for a minute," her friend said. "You're not looking too good."

"Just give me a minute. I don't have time to sit down. There's too much to do, and like you said, it would be best if I'm out of here before any news crews show up at the gate."

"I know, but you can spare a minute or five," Dannette said and went back to pulling items off the shelves, as if knowing what things Viviana wanted to take and what she didn't.

Viviana placed her hands on the dressing table for support. "I have so many emotions swirling around inside of me, and I can't seem to settle on one. I don't even know where to start with everything. This is...a lot to deal with. I'm packing to get out of here, but where should I go? I thought about moving into one of the suites at the hotel, but what if Thomas has set it up to where I'm banned from the property upon his death. I won't know much of anything until after I talk to Walter."

"You kept up your end of the agreement with him. You didn't step out on him. You pretended to be the dutiful wife, and you helped make that casino what it is today. A major success!" Dannette said with her hands on her hips. "Whoever has the final word would be a fool to remove you from your position. As for Thomas—I'm sure the bastard left plenty to you, including this house. I for one can't wait to find out what you're going to walk away with."

Viviana wasn't as optimistic. Dannette only knew what little Viviana had shared about her situation, and that was minimal. She also only knew Thomas from what she'd garnered while working for the company. She didn't know just how much of a ruthless bastard he really was. Viviana wouldn't be surprised if he hadn't left her anything.

He didn't give a damn about me. I was just a means to an end, she wanted to tell her friend but instead kept her mouth shut.

"In the meantime, you can stay with me," Dannette said. "My place isn't as lavish as you're accustomed to, and you have to cook and clean for yourself."

Her grin made Viviana smile. "I think I can handle all of that, and I'm going to take you up on the offer."

She had a beautiful condo not too far from the Las Vegas Strip that would be much more convenient for Viviana getting to and from work.

That was, assuming she'd still have a job.

"I'll only stay a few days. At least until I know where I stand as far as Thomas's estate. I have some money saved, but I don't want to touch much of it until I know what happens next."

As part of the prenup that she'd signed upon being forced to marry him, she would be entitled to a hundred thousand dollars for each year of their marriage. Which was seven years. That was chump change, considering Thomas was a billionaire. At least her job at the casino had paid well. Between her savings and investments, she'd been able to amass five hundred thousand dollars over the last few years.

It brought her some level of comfort knowing that, even if Thomas left her nothing, and she lost her job, at least she wouldn't be destitute. With the money she'd get from the prenup and her savings, she'd have enough to start over and decide her next steps.

All she had to do was get through the next few days—but Viviana had a feeling that things were going to get worse before they got better.

Chapter Two

"Oh! Oh! I can't believe he made that shot!" the basketball announcer screamed, and the crowd in the arena went wild. "Another three-pointer and that's number twelve from Hunter Graham tonight! He's having a record-breaking evening with forty-three points, thirteen rebounds, and eleven assists and there's still two minutes on the clock. Los Angeles has 108 points and Philadelphia 101. Philly still has time to..."

Franklin "Frankie" Evans sat in the third row, center court of the arena watching the Los Angeles Rivers play the last game of the NBA finals. The noise level was off the charts, and if the hometown team won—which it looked like they would— the fans were going to go crazy.

He had to admit that it had been an excellent game. Actually, the whole series had been a nail-biter with the teams tied three-three coming into game seven. And by the looks of it, there was a good chance that the Rivers would take home the finals' trophy. It also meant that he and some of his customers would make a shitload of money in the process. While others would be mad as hell.

As a bookie, Frankie lived for moments like this. The Los Angeles Rivers hadn't been expected to win. Hell, it was a shock they'd made it to the finals at all, considering their crap regular season. But there was a good chance that they were going to win the finals. He had taken in an obscene number of bets and with this game. The fees he charged alone would put an extra million dollars into his pockets.

He slouched down in his seat, stretched his legs out in front of him and folded his arms.

I love my life.

He always enjoyed a good game, but that wasn't his main reason for attending tonight. His sole purpose for being in the arena was because of Hunter Graham. The superstar player who owed him three hundred and fifty thousand dollars from previous bets on a boxing match and a baseball game.

The problem wasn't that Hunter owed him, the guy could afford it easily, but Frankie's issue with the multimillionaire was that he was taking his time paying him. If Hunter was anyone else, Frankie would rough him up good or cause him to have an unfortunate accident.

But Hunter Graham was the sport's world golden boy.

There was no way he could kill the bastard. He'd never get away with it. Hunter was well connected, and the world, especially the sport's world, loved him. There were always eyes on him. Besides, Frankie had made a lot of money off of the guy, despite the basketball star claiming he didn't have a gambling addiction. But when you owed a bookie two hundred thousand for a boxing debt and another hundred and fifty thousand after betting on the Yankees, who had gotten blown out the other day, you were addicted.

Frankie had never had a problem with Hunter paying.

Hell, the man was worth an obscene amount of money. He made at least five hundred thousand dollars a game, easily. He could afford his gambling habit, but Frankie just didn't like the guy. The man was arrogant and thought he was untouchable. That's why they needed to teach him a lesson.

Yeah, I need to put the fear of God in him.

Frankie elbowed the huge man sitting to his right. It was Bryce, one of his enforcers.

"Yeah, boss?"

"Make sure Vixen gets our boy Hunter to visit the strip club tonight. I need to talk to him," Frankie said, only speaking loud enough for Bryce to hear him. He had to raise his voice a little because of the fans chanting *Hunter, Hunter.*

Bryce nodded. Frankie then got Keith's attention—another enforcer—sitting to his left.

Keith leaned over. "Yeah?"

"Make sure you get Hunter's attention before we leave. I don't care how you do it. I want him to know that we were here tonight. We're going to have to start putting a little pressure on him to pay up."

Hunter was the type of person who had to learn things the hard way, and Frankie was just the man to teach him. Everyone had a weak spot. He would just have to find Hunter's.

I won't kill the guy, but I'll make him sorry he ever screwed with me.

* * *

"This was a good idea, but I can barely keep my eyes open," Scott, one of Hunter's teammates, said.

"I feel you, man." Hunter glanced out of the tinted window just before their driver opened the back door of the Chevy Suburban. It was one o'clock in the morning, and after running up and down the basketball court for almost the entire game, and celebrating with the team, his mind and body was spent. "But when Vixen calls and says there's a special show planned for me, it's hard not to show up."

"That's the only reason I came here with you two," Ricardo, another teammate, said as they walked into the dark building.

Visiting a strip club hadn't been a part of Hunter's plans for the evening. But after winning his second NBA Finals and the MVP, he was ready to cut loose. It didn't matter that the adrenaline from earlier had started to wane. He knew seeing Vixen dance, especially a private dance, which she had promised, was all he'd need to get his engine roaring again.

He couldn't remember the last time he'd stepped foot in *Stroke Me Gentleman's Club*. The NBA basketball season had been long and grueling. Between exhausting workouts, long practices, followed by the games, Hunter barely had enough energy to drag himself home or to a hotel. The last thing he'd wanted lately was to hang out at a bar or clubs.

"Congrats on the game!"

"Finals winners in the house!" Bouncers and others near the entrance spoke at once, congratulating them as they strolled in.

Winning game seven still seemed surreal. Considering all the talent in the NBA, getting to the finals was always a privilege. Actually winning, though, was a dream come true...again. But as congratulations continued coming their way, the reality was sinking in. The Los Angeles Rivers were the national champs.

They strolled further into the barely-lit club, and the bass in the music was playing so loud Hunter's insides were vibrating. Vixen had promised that his favorite table, center stage, would be available, and they headed that way. They skirted around customers and half-naked servers until they reached their destination.

"Hey, handsome. Good to see you again," a tall blonde said and smiled up at him while she served drinks to a table next to theirs. "I'll be right with you guys."

"Good," Hunter said as his gaze traveled over her black satin bra-like top that barely contained her double-D's. The short bandage-like skirt that she had squeezed into didn't cover much either. In fact, the bottom of her ass cheeks hung beneath the garment. A garter belt, fishnet stockings, and red platform stripper heels completed the outfit. Most of the other women working the floor were dressed similarly.

"All right, let's get this party started," Ricardo said, pulling a wad of cash from his pants pocket and making it rain toward the stage.

Minutes later, Hunter and the guys had drinks in hand while Ms. Cotton Candy performed on stage. She was grooving to Drake's, "Way 2 Sexy" and had stripped down to nothing but a bubble gum pink thong and matching high heels. The woman was cute and extremely flexible as she slid to the floor in a split and leaned back, revealing the goodies between her thighs. But she wasn't the person Hunter was there to see.

He glanced around the semi-dark packed space, hoping to get a glimpse of Vixen. Instead, there were numerous strippers making their rounds throughout the room, getting customers sexually worked up and giving lap dances.

But where was Vixen?

Shortly after the thought filled his mind, someone stepped in front of him, blocking his view of the stage.

"Hot damn," Scott murmured and the three of them sat up straighter with their mouths hanging open.

Vixen lived up to her name. She was at least six feet tall with large breasts, a tiny waist and hips that flared just enough to give her an hourglass figure...and legs that went on forever, accentuated with sky-high heels.

Good Lord.

Hunter's gaze worked its way up her slammin' body, and he took in her outfit. She was dressed in a black leather dominatrix outfit that made it clear that she'd had a Brazilian wax recently. The little strap of material between her thighs wasn't hiding much, and the way the garment was made, he didn't have to look at her ass to know that it was hanging out. That was the same when it came to the cut outs that gave a clear view of her large breasts.

Hunter released a groan and shifted in his seat. His jeans suddenly grew tighter as his dick pressed against his zipper. She definitely knew how to get a rise out of him with her sexy-ass body on full display.

Vixen was *fiiiine*, but what made her stand out, once you got to know her, was that she had brains to go along with that pretty face. Her body was a work of art—but it was a shame she'd had to resort to stripping to pay her way through law school. She could be so much more.

If Hunter was looking to settle down with one woman—which he wasn't—Vixen would be a contender. Then again, maybe not. He'd had dinner with her once outside of the Strip club, and she was smart and engaging. He just couldn't get past the fact that she was a stripper. She had tried to pursue something more with him, but he'd shot that down real quick.

He wasn't looking for anything serious. Hell, he wasn't even looking for anything casual these days, because in his experience, women couldn't do casual. They wanted more from him. Most of the time their main interest was about the life he could give them and nothing more.

Yet, there had been one time when he'd found the real thing—a woman who loved him for him. A woman he had wanted to spend the rest of his life with. The only woman he had ever loved and would love.

But never again.

He would never be that stupid again.

As for Vixen, he liked her, but they had never gone further than her performing oral sex on him. There had never been any kissing, except for when she kissed his cheek or neck. Nothing more than that could ever happen between them.

Besides, there was no way he'd ever settle down with a stripper.

Despite what others thought and the way the media portrayed him, getting photos of him with some of the most beautiful women in the world, he was most attracted to the girl-next-door types. If he was ever going to settle down, it would be with a good girl—one he'd be comfortable taking home to meet his mother, not a woman who put her body on display for a living. He didn't care how sexually attractive she was. It would never happen.

Vixen planted her hands on her hips, and pulled him out of his thoughts when her ruby-red lips lifted into a sensual smile.

"Welcome back," she said to Hunter, and stepped forward before straddling his lap.

Her intoxicating scent wafted to his nose and scrambled his brain. Everything about the woman was sexy, and he was here for it. She didn't acknowledge his buddies at all, and Hunter didn't care. What he wanted to do was carry her to one of the private rooms and let her have her way with him.

"Congratulations on your big win." She boldly peppered kisses down the side of his neck as her hands slowly glided up his torso before she leaned in close to his ear. "How about we go in back and celebrate?"

Without waiting for a response, she climbed off of him and reached for his hand. She'd guided him away before he'd had a chance to tell his guys that he'd be back. She led him to the rear of the club toward the private rooms, which was good. He was in need of sexual release, and she was the perfect person to give it to him. Her lap dances were legendary.

"I'm glad you were able to come tonight."

"I'm planning on coming several times if my experience with you is like usual."

Vixen laughed. The throaty sound had his body throbbing with need, and she hadn't even danced for him yet.

She pushed open the door to a room that was lit by a crimson light bulb, giving the area a sexy vibe. Hunter dropped down on the long red leather sofa and reached for Vixen, who came to him willingly.

"You're as beautiful as ever," he said as he scooted down in his seat and started unbuckling his belt, but Vixen stopped him with a hand on his.

"Don't," she said in a whisper, and Hunter frowned, but before he could say anything, she leaned in close to his ear. To anyone watching, it probably looked as if she was kissing his neck. "I'm so sorry about this, but he threatened to fire me, and I need this job."

Hunter froze.

He didn't have to ask *who*.

Frankie, his bookie, was part owner of the club. The man wasn't above threatening or blackmailing anyone to get what he wanted. That only made Hunter want to hold out even longer from paying him. If the asshole thought he could force money out of him, he had another thing coming.

The door opened at the same time the thought entered his mind, and Frankie strolled in. He had a lit cigar in his hand and one of his goons by his side.

"Surely you didn't think you could walk up in my club

without me knowing," he said to Hunter, then turned to Vixen. "Get out of here, Vixen."

Vixen glanced at Hunter, worry in her eyes as she mouthed the word *sorry*. She hurried out the door, closing it behind her.

Yeah, he was sorry, too—sorry that he hadn't taken his ass home after partying with the guys at the arena. This was just another reminder that he needed to get his shit together and start making better decisions.

Hunter huffed out a breath and crossed his leg, placing one ankle on his knee while he draped his arms on the back of the sofa. Frankie was the type of person who thrived on other's fear. Hunter hadn't expected to see him at the club, even though he had spotted the short bald man and his goons sitting close behind his team after they'd won.

But Hunter had been so caught up in the celebration, he hadn't given them a second thought.

He stared Frankie down. The man couldn't be more than five feet seven with a slim build and a slight beer belly. Hunter was almost taller than him even while sitting. If it weren't for Frankie's full beard that Hunter knew hid a long scar that went from his ear to the middle of his chin, he'd look like a twelve-year-old.

They had a similar complexion but while Hunter was mixed race—black mother and a white biological father—both of Frankie's parents were black. Rumor had it he'd grown up in the roughest part of Compton and had to fight to stay alive daily because of all the gang activity in his neighborhood. He might've been wealthy now and had moved far away from his old stomping grounds, but the man was still a mean son of a bitch.

Hunter could've paid him by now, and probably would've already, but he didn't like people telling him what to do. He was Hunter-Fucking-Graham, one of the top ten players in

NBA history. He was also one of the wealthiest professional athletes ever, and Frankie knew this.

Frankie also knew Hunter was good for the money. He always paid.

"You have a lot of nerve coming to my club when you owe me money," the short man said as he puffed on his cigar and blew the smoke toward the ceiling as if there wasn't a law about smoking inside the building. He sat on the far end of the sofa.

Frankie had what many would call the little-man complex. He was always to flex and intimidate to overcompensate for his small stature. He also rarely went anywhere without at least two bodyguards who doubled as enforcers.

Hunter couldn't much blame him in his line of work. Being a bookie, Frankie had to deal with a lot of shady characters.

"You're in debt to me for three hundred and fifty thousand dollars. Yet, you walked in here like you didn't have a care in the world, even though you haven't made any effort to pay me. Why is that?"

"Man, I've been busy," Hunter said, exhaustion starting to catch up to him.

"You're not busy now. Where's my damn money?"

"Come on now, Frankie. You know I'm good for it. Don't worry. I got you. Now why don't you leave and send Vixen back in here. You're messing up my buzz."

Hunter was done with Vixen and only said that to get a rise out of the bookie.

Frankie bolted out of his seat and stood a couple of feet in front of Hunter. "You and this fucked-up world might think you're all that, but to *me*, you're just another asshole who owes me money. And I'm losing patience."

Hunter wasn't afraid of the little squirt. As a matter of fact, Frankie wasn't anything but an irritating gnat that he wished he could swat away.

Was the scowl he had on his ruddy face supposed to intimidate him? Hunter had to hold back a laugh. Clearly the jerk had forgotten that it was people like Hunter who'd made him as wealthy as he was.

Hunter stood and Keith, the enforcer, who was close to Hunter's height but had about thirty pounds on him, moved closer to Frankie's side.

Hunter fought the smile struggling to break free. Surely, they didn't think he was going to try and fight them, especially not over a few hundred thousand dollars. Hell, he made more than that every minute of the day.

"You ready to pay up?" Frankie asked, irritation dangling from each word.

"Like I said last week when you confronted me, I'll take care of you after the season. We just finished tonight. At least let me catch my breath. You know I'm good for the money. Why are you sweating me so much? Are you that hard up for cash?"

Frankie moved forward and Hunter stood his ground. He wasn't a fighter, but he knew how to handle himself. His brother, Malik, a former Navy SEAL and the owner of Supreme Security, a personal security company in Chicago and Atlanta, had made sure of that.

But fighting was the last thing Hunter wanted to do right now. The media was already hounding him about his gambling hobby, to the point of the NBA investigating him a second time a few months back. The last thing he needed was for the NBA to find out that he'd got into it with a bookie, but still...

"Listen, I'm going to pay you. Just let me catch my breath, man. Besides, I'll probably be ready to put a wager on the Yankee's game next week."

Hunter already knew that Frankie wouldn't send him away. He'd made too much money off of him. Actually, they'd both made plenty of money, but lately, Hunter had been on a losing streak. He didn't expect it to last much longer, though.

"You have three days or else," Frankie ground out, his face red with anger.

Hunter's own anger rose to the surface. He took a step forward. "You're threatening me?"

Keith shoved Hunter's shoulder. "Back the hell up."

"Get off of me. I'm asking a question," Hunter said to the hired help, but glared at Frankie. "You threatening me? We've had dealings for years, and now you want to threaten me?"

"Just get out of here and get my money," Frankie said with less force.

"Yeah, I thought so. Your ass needs me and my connections. I suggest you remember that the next time you come at me. I'll get your money."

When I'm damn good and ready, Hunter thought that last part, but didn't speak the words.

"Let's go," Keith said, gripping Hunter's arm a little too tight for comfort, and Hunter shook him off.

He strolled out of the room with no intentions of ever stepping foot in the place again. As he made his way back to the front of the building, he spotted Vixen near the door of another room. She called out to him, but he kept walking as if he didn't hear her. He was done with her too.

Hell, he should've been done with her months ago.

He needed to make some changes, but first, this might be a good time to take a trip.

Las Vegas, here I come.

Chapter Three

Viviana nervously gripped the steering wheel of her Hyundai Kona electric car as she maneuvered through the streets of Henderson, Nevada. She hadn't driven much over the years since Thomas had insisted on her having a driver. If they'd been in a loving marriage, she would've assumed it was because he wanted her protected.

But Viviana knew better than that.

She was fairly sure he'd only done it to keep tabs on her. Then again, he was so unpredictable. Maybe he really had been concerned about her safety. Being married to a wealthy man made her a target, though she'd never had any serious, life-threatening scares. Still, after saving enough money, a year ago she had purchased her own car without much pushback from Thomas.

She only drove it for a few appointments, like the hair salon and to get her nails done. Outside of that, a driver took her everywhere she wanted to go, including to work.

Until this week.

Since Thomas's death, she'd depended on herself to get

around. Granted, she'd only driven from Dannette's house to work and back again every day, but she was finally flexing her independence.

And her nervous energy had nothing to do with lack of driving, but everything to do with the fact that she was on her way to Thomas's lawyer's office. Attorney Walter Underwood had asked her to come for the reading of the will.

The last few days had been some of the longest of Viviana's life. The day of Thomas's death, after talking with the management staff at work, she'd spoken with a reporter. She had given the woman a brief statement, basically confirming that Thomas had died of a heart attack earlier that morning.

Though the woman bombarded her with one question after another regarding the hotel, the casino, and a few other companies that Thomas owned, Viviana hadn't been able to answer the questions. At the time, she'd had no idea what would happen to the businesses, or any of Thomas's properties, including the home she'd lived in.

Needless to say, it had been a very short interview. Their marriage wasn't conventional, and though Viviana had some knowledge of a few of Thomas's assets, she was sure there was so much she didn't know.

Viviana had arranged a memorial service for Thomas that took place yesterday. She had reluctantly done it, but hadn't attended the service. What would've been the point? There was no way she could've pretended that she was mourning the loss of her husband. She wasn't. She wouldn't have been able to stomach listening to people go on and on about how wonderful, generous, or kind Thomas had been.

Mainly because she hadn't experienced that with him.

To the outside world, they'd been a somewhat happily married couple who put on a good front when out together. In reality, there marriage was in name only, and even the name part wasn't real. She'd gone by Viviana Reagan, but as part of their marriage contract, she had insisted on two things: she got to keep her name and no sex. Everything else, she felt she could handle.

"It's almost over," she mumbled to herself when she reached the Green Valley Ranch district and followed the GPS instructions to the law office.

It had been five long days since Thomas's death, and Viviana couldn't wait to get the will reading over with. She'd been living in limbo for days now and good or bad, she was ready to meet with Walter about the fate of her life.

A short while later, after parking in the structure, she headed to the elevators. Within minutes, she was stepping out on the fifth floor, and immediately upon seeing the sign *Law Office of Walter Underwood*, memories flooded her mind.

Viviana swallowed hard. She clutched the handle of her Chanel bag tighter as if it were a lifeline. All the while remembering the first time she'd been in front of the heavy-looking wood door. It had been the day she'd signed the marriage contract.

One of the worse days of her life.

Her breathing increased, and the fear, anger, and defeat she had felt then came rushing back. She remained standing in the middle of the carpeted hallway staring at the closed door. It was taking all of her willpower not to turn on her heels and return to the elevators.

Just calm down. Relax. You've got this. You're free.

Remembering that, she released a noisy breath and willed herself to move forward. The moment she pushed open the door, a younger woman with red, wavy hair and light brown eyes glanced up at her. She was sitting behind a long counter.

"Hi. May I help you?" she said, flashing a friendly smile that helped Viviana relax a little more.

"Hi. I'm Viviana Conn..." she started, but caught herself. "Reagan. I'm Viviana Reagan here to see Attorney Underwood."

"Ahh, yes, Mrs. Reagan. He's expecting you. Right this way."

Viviana followed her down the long hallway, and passed a couple of offices where she could hear people talking behind closed doors. The woman didn't stop until they reached the last door on the end. She knocked and a muffled voice told them to come in.

"Mrs. Reagan is here for her appointment."

Walter Underwood, an older gentleman with a full head of salt-and-pepper hair, placed the glasses he was wearing on the desk and stood. He flashed a quick smile which Viviana could barely see behind his mustache and full beard.

"Thanks, Yancy. That'll be all," he said. His soft-spoken voice didn't match his tall frame and large build.

The woman nodded and backed out of the office, closing the door behind her.

"Good seeing you again, Viviana. Please, have a seat." He gestured to one of the chairs in front of the desk. "We're waiting for one more person, and then we'll get started. In the meantime, can I get you something to drink? Water, tea, coffee?"

"A bottle of water would be great," she said and claimed her seat.

"Thanks for coming." He handed her the bottle of water before returning to his seat. "I know how busy you are, and I'll try not to keep you too long. How are you holding up?"

Viviana unscrewed the top on the water as she debated on how to answer. "It's been...an interesting few days, but I'm hanging in there."

"I know none of this...arrangement has been easy for you.

Just so that you know, based on the terms of the agreement, you have upheld your part and will receive all that was promised to you." He glanced at the platinum watch on his wrist and frowned.

"Hopefully, Mr—" His words were cut off when there was a knock at the door. "Come in."

"Mr. Graham is here, sir."

Viviana had just taken a swig of water when she glanced over her shoulder and saw the last person she ever expected to see. She swallowed wrong and a coughing fit had her leaning forward while she pounded against her chest. Tears filled her eyes as she struggled to catch her breath.

"Viviana?" Attorney Underwood hurried to her side and patted her back. "Are you okay? Do you need..."

She waved him off, batted tears away, and finally looked back at the door, thinking that maybe she'd been seeing things.

Nope. He was still standing there. The man who she had walked away from seven years ago. The man who she had never been able to forget. And the man she had never stopped loving.

"Hunter?" she croaked.

Viviana couldn't stop staring. It was one thing to see Hunter on TV running up and down a basketball court. But it was another thing to see the real live version of him standing only a few feet away looking downright delectable.

Gone was the young man she'd first fallen in love with during college, and in his place was a drool-worthy Adonis who was sure to turn heads everywhere he went. Not just because of his 6'6" height, but because the broad-shouldered physically-fit man was downright *fiine*.

He used to wear his dark wavy hair pulled back in a ponytail. Not anymore. Now his hair was cut close to his head, giving him a more mature appearance. His fair skin, courtesy of his mixed-race, glowed a pale gold and highlighted a few more freckles around his nose than she'd remembered.

Her gaze traveled lower. Viviana wasn't sure if he just hadn't shaved or if the light scruff on his cheek and chin was him growing a full beard. Either way, it only added to his sexiness.

Her gaze went back to his midnight-dark eyes, and then she frowned, remembering they were in Walter's office.

"Hunter...what are you doing here?"

* * *

Hunter wasn't sure how long he stood there, staring at the woman he hadn't ever planned to see again. Sure, he knew there was a chance that she might be at the meeting, but actually seeing her face to face was more jarring than he'd expected.

He was surrounded by beautiful women all the time, but to this day, none had ever been as stunning as Viviana...his ex-fiancée.

God, she had crushed him when she walked away from what they'd had...what they'd been building. At the time, it had been like she had reached into his chest, ripped out his heart, and then slammed it against a wall. Yet, Hunter couldn't take his gaze off of her. He had always been attracted to dark, mocha sisters, and Viviana's satiny skin, a stark contrast to his lighter tone, glistened under the florescent lights.

As usual, her hair was perfectly styled. Back at UC Berkeley, and even years later after they were engaged, she wore a bob that stopped at her shoulders. Today her jet-black hair was cut into a short style where the sides and back were low. The top was long and so was her bang that was swept to the side, practically covering her right eye. It was sexy as hell and only enhanced her gorgeous round face.

Then there were her chestnut brown eyes. Like when they were in college, Hunter couldn't look away. There was so much emotion radiating in those dark orbs as she stared back at him. His gaze lowered to her mouth, and he groaned internally when her tongue swiped across her lower lip.

Good Lord, those soft-looking sweet lips that he used to feast on were just as tempting as they'd been all those years ago. *Damn. Damn. Damn.*

Why now? Why did he have to run into her today? Especially when exhaustion from a long basketball season had finally caught up to him. He was dog-tired and his defenses weren't as strong as he needed them to be around her.

Someone cleared their throat, and Hunter's gaze shifted to the man who was standing near the desk.

"If you'll come in and have a seat, Mr. Graham, we can get started," the attorney said as he sat in his leather chair and shuffled a stack of papers.

Hunter didn't say anything. Instead, he took the seat next to Viviana, and immediately her heady scent of lavender with a hint of vanilla swirled around him, tempting him to lean in close for a better whiff.

His brother had always tortured him in one way or another, and now he was doing it from the grave by insisting Hunter be at the reading of his will.

Asshole.

"We'll get started. I'll read this portion of the will before I give you the letters that Thomas left for each of you."

Hunter barely listened as the attorney read a statement that apparently his brother had written about being sorry for what he'd put Hunter and Viviana through. He claimed that he had his reasons for what he'd done to each of them, even if they were self-serving.

Hunter grunted in disgust, and the longer he sat there

listening to his brother's words, the more he wanted to get up and walk out. But what kept him rooted in place was curiosity. His stepbrother hated him; at least that's what Hunter had assumed.

Why else would Thomas lure Viviana away from him and then marry her?

"To my only brother and my wife," Walter was saying when Hunter tuned back in, "I leave to you TGR Grand Hotel and Casino to be shared equally, fifty-fifty. To my wife..."

Hunter sat stunned as the attorney continued.

What. The. Hell. Thomas left me TGR Grand?

Had he really heard that right? The casino and hotel were easily valued in the billions. There had to be a catch. No way would Thomas treat him like shit from the time Hunter was ten years old until the day he stole his fiancée.

"Wait?" Hunter interrupted. "Back up. Did I hear you correctly? Thomas left his casino, the thing he cherished more than anything, to me? I mean, to both of us?"

"That's correct, Mr. Graham. He also left letters for both of you." Walter handed each of them a white envelope. "We've come to the moment to where he wanted you both to read your letters."

Hunter knew Thomas. He might not have seen him in seven years, but he knew the low-down dirty dog. There was no way the man left him a casino without there being a huge catch. He probably set the whole thing to blow the moment Hunter stepped inside the place.

Hunter braced himself as he opened the envelope and pulled out the letter. He was surprised to see it actually in his brother's handwriting.

What's up, my brother?

If you're reading this, that means I'm on my way to heaven. Ha ha ha. That also means that you know that I left you half of the casino. *You're probably wondering—what's the catch? There isn't one. Seriously. Well, not really.*

I should be thanking you. It's because of you, indirectly, that I worked my ass off to become a successful billionaire. I wanted to prove to my father that I was just as good as you. I might not have had your athleticism, but I had a good business mind that has served me well.

I've been doing a lot of soul-searching this past year, and believe it or not, for the most part, I'm sorry for what I did to you and Viviana. I'll admit that I've always been angry and a little jealous of you. My father and I never had a super-strong bond before he died, but before you came along, we at least hung out. But then you showed up with basketball skills that could rival someone twice your age. I ain't mad at you for that, but I hate you for taking my father from me.

You were everything I wasn't in his eyes—tall, good-looking, and a future NBA star. Your love of sports and athletic abilities bonded the two of you and destroyed anything he and I had. Which was why I took something—or should I say someone— you loved. She was way out of your league, anyway.

Now that I'm gone, you can have Viviana back. She served her purpose. Good luck with that, though. Assuming you'll ever be interested in her again, she probably won't give you the time of day. Not because I'm the better brother, though I am, but because your stupid ass has a gambling problem.

Ha ha ha. Yeah, I know about that. The gambling world is small, my brother, and word on the street is that you'll probably end up broke since you bet on everything. The stupidest things...

Anyway, Viviana will never want you mainly because of that. I wish I could be there to watch her crush your spirits again. I guess I'll just have to watch from the sidelines. Oh, and good luck with that trifling mother of hers. I wouldn't be

*surprised if after seven years, Chandra starts showing her face
again.*

Enjoy the benefits of owning a casino. It has served me well.

Thomas.

Hunter's heart was beating so fast and hard, everyone in
the office could probably hear it. He hadn't realized he had
balled the letter up in his hand, but when he noticed he had, he
tossed it on the attorney's desk.

"Sell my half of the casino as soon as possible. I want my
inheritance in cash," he blurted, and jerked out of his seat,
causing the chair to fall backward. He stormed out of the office,
wanting nothing to do with anything that once belonged to
Thomas.

And that included Viviana.

Chapter Four

He hates me, Viviana thought as Hunter stormed out of the office.

Who could blame him? She had professed her love, promised to marry him, and then walked away with no explanation and married his stepbrother. Granted, she hadn't been able to tell him the truth—and he should've known that she wouldn't have walked away without a good reason—still, she had hurt him.

Attorney Underwood picked up the phone and spoke quietly into the receiver. The only words that Viviana was able to make out was, *stop him from leaving.*

Hunter had every right to be angry and to hate her. What she'd done to him had been unforgivable. But that hadn't stopped her body from coming alive the moment he had stepped into the office. That had never happened with her husband, or any other man for that matter.

The last seven years she'd lived like a nun and hadn't even wanted to look at another man. She'd felt nothing but numbness whenever she was near Thomas. She just knew she was dead inside. Yet, the moment her and Hunter's gazes collided, all of the old feelings from years ago came rushing back. He still had a visceral effect on her with the ability to stir desire that she'd only ever had for him.

It also let her know that she was very much alive inside.

Goodness.

This wasn't good. Nothing about seeing him was good. Not the way her body responded to his nearness, and not the fact that she had to share a casino with him. She didn't know what was more shocking—that Thomas had left them his billion-dollar casino, or that he expected them to share it.

But what the heck was she going to do since Hunter wanted to sell his half?

She had worked her ass off to help build Thomas's empire. Hell, as far as she was concerned, she'd earned the right to own one hundred percent of the business. After the long days and nights, tears, and headache that had gone into making the casino one of the best in the country, no way was she just going to let Hunter sell it. She loved the place, the people, and most importantly, she loved her job.

Viviana sighed. She couldn't afford to buy Hunter out, and the thought of sharing a casino—a casino that she had made into what it was today—with someone she didn't know was daunting. That person would have a say in how the organization was ran.

And what if they wanted to change all of the systems that she had meticulously put into place?

"He's not returning," she said to Walter when he hung up the phone. "Let's just move forward, and maybe I...or you...can give him a call later."

Walter gave her a slow nod. "Have you read the letter?"

Viviana had temporarily forgotten about the letter in her hand. "No."

"I'll need you to read it before I continue."

She nodded even though she was fairly sure she didn't want to hear or read anything Thomas had to say. Then again, he'd just left her and Hunter his casino. Surely, there was a catch, and she'd rather know what it was now before she got too excited.

She unfolded the letter.

Dear wifey,

If you're reading this, that means I've died before you and before the end of our marriage contract. Pity. I had planned to outlive you. With that said, it's been...real. I've enjoyed parts of our collaboration. Yes, that's how I'm referring to our joke of a marriage.

You're probably shocked that I took the time to write you a letter. I'll admit, Walter made me do it. He thought it was the least I could do after what I put you through. Whatever. Now that I've started writing, though, it's not as bad of an assignment as I first thought.

So let me start with the good. You're a smart woman, Viviana. I recognized that the first time I met you at one of my stepmother's Christmas parties. I was shocked that a jock like Hunter could hold the attention of someone as intelligent as you.

In that moment, I wanted you for my own. I needed a good woman by my side, and I chose you.

Problem was, you were crazy in love with my sneaker-headed brother. You even agreed to marry the loser, but I wasn't giving up. Especially when I found out that you guys were going to have a long engagement because of you going to grad school and his career. Anyway, I got you. Granted it wasn't quite what I had in mind, but still. I took you from him and that was worth everything I had to invest.

I never thanked you for all that you did for my business. I can admit that when you came to work for me at the casino, I had my doubts on whether you could make a difference, but you proved me wrong. You accepted the director of operations position and made it your own. You took your role seriously and made the casino even more profitable than I could've imagine. And though I know we had our differences, I trusted you with the company, and you didn't let me down. Thanks for that, which is why I thought it only fair that you have the casino.

See, I'm not a total asshole. On top of that, I'm throwing in the hotel as well, because it's just easier. Who knows, maybe you can turn it around and get it to run as smoothly as the casino. God knows that Xavier hasn't been able to do that. He might've been my best friend, but he's a lousy manager. I probably should've canned him a long time ago, but there were some areas he was good at. He knows his stuff, but... Anyway, he's your problem now.

Just so we're clear, the hotel and casino are all you're getting from me. I know how much you love the house we lived in, but I'm leaving it to someone else—my baby's momma.

Viviana's breath caught, and she reread the sentence, shocked that Thomas had a child and never mentioned it. Then again, why should she be shocked? She wasn't having sex with him. She should've assumed he was getting his needs met by someone.

As for the house, good riddance.

After releasing a slow, steadying breath, she continued reading.

Yep, you heard me right. Since your frigid ass wasn't giving me any, I sought release elsewhere. For over a year, I honored my marriage vow to you. I preferred not to be one of those guys who slept around, but after a year of celibacy, I was done waiting. I gave you everything, provided and protected you because we had an agreement. I know you insisted that sex not be a part of the agreement. Yet, I thought you'd change your mind.

Anyway, it doesn't matter. For the last six years, I had a good time and got a kid out of it. He's almost a year old, and he and his mother will be well taken care of. Don't worry, you'll never hear from her. She has strict instructions to stay clear of you or she'll lose everything.

I know you thought I was a monster, but I protected you from more than you realize. But you're on your own now. I'm sure you're happy about that. Enjoy your newfound freedom. Just know that when people learn just how wealthy you are, you're going to wish I was around to provide protection.

Oh, and if you think my self-absorbed, arrogant brother will have your back, you can think again. He might be a grown man, but he doesn't know the first thing about how to take care of a woman. He sure as hell doesn't know how to run a business. Which is why he is part-owner of the hotel and casino. We'll see how good you are at running the businesses with extra dead-weight on your team. Then again, the partnership will never work. He hates you too much to work with you, and you're too laden with guilt to work with him.

As for getting Hunter back? That'll never happen. He's not the forgiving type, and he probably has too many gorgeous women willing to open their legs for him. Unlike you, who is as frigid as they come. It's a shame to have let that sexy body go to waste, but your loss.

This next year should be interesting. Damn, I wish I was there in person to watch. Well, anyway, I can imagine how this is going to go.

Also, now that you're rich, I'm sure your mother will be coming back around. Good luck with that. Hopefully, you're better able to handle her than you were back in the day. Not! Ha ha ha. Oh, and getting back to my brother, I hope he appreciates the sacrifice you made for him all those years ago. He still thinks he's invincible, but I'm sure someone will put him in his place eventually.

Until we meet again.

Thomas

Viviana didn't realize she was crying until she felt something wet on her cheek. They weren't tears of sadness, but of anger. Just when she thought she couldn't hate Thomas anymore, he went and brought up her mother.

As for leaving her and Hunter the hotel and casino—damn him for putting her in this position. It was bad enough that he had destroyed her life and forced her to live the last seven years with him. But to make her have to work with Hunter, after forcing her to betray him, was just cruel.

"Here you go," Walter said, offering her a tissue box.

She snatched a few sheets of tissue and thanked him. Wiping her face, her mind raced with so many thoughts and questions. Her number-one concern was holding onto the hotel and casino. How could she do that without buying Hunter out?

But then she thought of something Thomas said in the letter. She looked at Walter.

"Thomas said this next year should be interesting. Why is that?" she asked.

Walter sighed. "If you or Hunter try and sell your portion of the hotel and casino within a year, you'll both walk away with nothing."

Viviana just stared at him. Either she had to figure out a way to work with Hunter and get him not to sell, or she could kiss billions of dollars and all of her hard work goodbye.

God! I hate you, Thomas.

Chapter Five

Hunter was lost in thought as his driver crept through traffic. His mind kept circling around all that had happened recently.

What a day. Hell, what a week.

After leaving the strip club the other night, he had planned to charter a plane and fly to Vegas for a few weeks, maybe even a month. He intended to rest his body, do a little gambling, and see what other fun and relaxation he could get into during the off season. But then Walter had called with the news about Thomas's death. A heart attack.

Now, days later, Hunter was trying to wrap his mind around everything.

I own a damn hotel and casino.

Hunter wasn't sure what was more mind-boggling: that, or the fact that he owned it with his ex-fiancée.

Seeing Viviana again had felt like an out-of-body experience. How many times had he fantasized about coming face-to-face with her? But nothing could've prepared him for the moment. Not only was she still as gorgeous as ever, but everything he'd once felt for her came rushing back like a tsunami crashing into the shore. Attraction. Desire. Longing. The moment their eyes connected it all hit him at once.

How the hell was that possible?

He despised her.

He hated her for the shit she'd put him through.

Yet, the desire he'd felt the moment he saw her in the office had knocked the breath out of him.

Hunter shook his head. *Unbelievable. It just doesn't make sense.*

Viviana had made a fool of him. How could he still be attracted to her?

She had walked out of his life, leaving only a note and the custom-made engagement ring that he'd given her a year earlier. What made it worse was that she had left him during the NBA playoffs.

Not only that, she'd done it the night before the biggest game of the season for him and his team. Because of her, they lost the first round of playoffs.

That was unforgiveable.

Hunter laid his head back and closed his eyes as the memories bombarded him. The series had been tied three to three and they were scheduled to play game seven the next night. They needed the win. They could've won. But his head hadn't been in the game. How could it be? After years of being together, she'd said goodbye with a note.

Viviana had been his heart. The only woman he'd ever loved. The woman he had planned to spend the rest of his life with. And she crushed his world with a damn goodbye note, telling him that she couldn't marry him. That, and for him not to call her or come looking for her.

Despite all of the distance and baggage between them, seeing Viviana again reminded him of the life they'd planned to build together. They'd been a helluva team and then, in an instant...they weren't.

Hunter opened his eyes and ran his hands down his face as he recalled how he'd gone out of his mind with worry for her. He had even hired a private investigator friend, Cameron "Wiz" Miller to find her.

But before Wiz could start the job, Thomas had called Hunter. His stepbrother had told him that he'd married Viviana.

Hunter had completely lost his shit, thinking he'd never recover from the loss of the only woman he'd ever loved.

Damn you, Thomas. Damn you!

Heart pounding hard as a new wave of fury roared inside of him, Hunter knew he needed to pull himself together. He had given Viviana and Thomas too much power over his thoughts and emotions years ago. He wasn't giving them that power today.

Hunter's gaze drifted outside when they pulled up to the gatehouse of the home he had rented. After confirming that it was him, the guard let them through the twelve-foot wrought iron gate. It matched the fencing that went around the whole property.

As they drove up the long double-wide driveway, the sprawling mega mansion with more windows than Hunter could count, came into view. This was home for the next couple of weeks.

After learning of Thomas's death, his mother wanted to travel with him and had decided to host a mini-family reunion while in Vegas. When she told him her idea, Hunter had his real estate agent find him a house to rent for a couple of weeks. The ten-bedroom, twelve-bathroom estate sat on almost two acres, and had all the luxuries of home. It would definitely be large enough to house everyone.

Only immediate family would be in attendance, including his biological brother, Malik, and his family. As well as honorary family members—Wiz and Quinn and their families —who were actually Malik's best friends. The guys were like brothers to Hunter, too, and though he looked forward to seeing them, right now he wanted to be alone.

I should've gone to the condo.

He owned a three-bedroom, three-bathroom condo near the Las Vegas Strip. It was what he usually used when in town, and he wished he'd thought of going there after leaving Walter's office. At least for a few hours. There was no doubt that his mother was going to bombard him with questions the moment he walked in.

A short while later, he dragged himself into the massive home, and stopped in the two-story foyer. An eye-catching crystal chandelier hung overhead and to his right was the spiral staircase. His home in LA was impressive and had been featured in *House Beautiful*, but this place was also a showpiece.

"Hunter? Is that you?" His mother's voice came from the kitchen, and he headed that way.

"Yeah, it's me." The home came with three efficient staff members and a cook, but they probably wouldn't have much to do since his mother didn't like to be waited on.

Hunter smiled when he entered the kitchen and saw his mother, Diane, and the cook sitting at the table drinking tea. No surprise there. She made a friend wherever she went, and no doubt she and the cook would be besties before they left.

The cook hurried to stand. "Mr. Graham, can I get you some lunch?"

"Nayma, you don't have to fuss over him," his mother said as she started clearing dishes from where they'd been sitting, and Hunter cocked an eyebrow at her.

Just because she didn't want anyone waiting on her didn't mean that he didn't. As much as he was paying, all he planned to do was take care of his personal needs. Everything else would be left to the staff to do, including cook and serve him. He wouldn't be mean about it, but he'd let them do the jobs they were hired to do.

"He's perfectly capable of fending for himself," his mother continued. "Son, there are sandwiches and salad in the refrigerator, but before you eat, let's talk."

"Actually, I'd rather eat than talk," he said, and rinsed his hands in the sink.

Despite what his mother said, Nayma pulled items out of the refrigerator and piled food onto a plate for him. Either her or his mother had also made a cheesecake loaded with strawberries on top—his favorite.

"Have a seat at the table, and I'll bring everything to you," Nayma instructed. "Would you like something to drink? I made freshly squeezed lemonade."

Hunter smirked at his mother when she scowled at him. "Sounds good. Thanks, Nayma. I appreciate you. Oh, and you can call me Hunter," he said, moments before biting into his hoagie.

She smiled and gave him a nod before leaving the kitchen.

"It was that bad, huh?" his mother asked gently and sat next to him at the round glass table.

Though he didn't consider himself a momma's boy, his mother was one of his biggest supporters. Despite her occasionally rocky life, one thing he never doubted was her love for him.

Before he came along, Diane had been a single mom to Malik. Hunter had been in middle school when she married Hunter's father, but then he passed away. Years later, she met and fell in love with Thomas's dad. They were married for five years until he died.

She'd had one loss after another, but her love for Hunter had never wavered.

"Yes. The meeting was that bad and loaded with a few shocks," he finally said.

He gave her a quick rundown of what had happened at the attorney's office, and even told her about the letter that Thomas had left him. As he recited what he could remember, he wondered what had been in Viviana's letter. Then again, he didn't really care. For his own protection, he needed to keep his distance. No way was he letting her near his heart again, and that meant not caring about anything that concerned her.

"Wow, the casino and hotel? I'm...shocked. For a person who clearly didn't like you, that's a very generous gift. Then again, that boy was always...different. Sometimes I just didn't understand him," Diane said thoughtfully.

Even with the rift between Hunter and his stepbrother, Diane and Thomas had a good relationship. She had even attended the man's memorial service. Initially, when she married Thomas's father, Hunter had been okay sharing her. But after the fiasco with Viviana, he hadn't wanted his mother anywhere near Thomas.

Diane had her own mind, though. She didn't cut all ties, claiming he needed her especially since his father had passed, which had been years ago. But ultimately, her allegiance was to Hunter—to a point. She never spoke Thomas's name around him, nor did they visit each other, but they kept in touch. The guy was always sending her lavish birthday, Mother's Day, and Christmas gifts. In turn, Diane, an amazing cook, often found a way to send Thomas some of his favorite dishes of hers, including a sour cream pound cake for his birthdays.

"I hope you weren't rude or mean to that young lady," his mother said, cutting into Hunter's thoughts and he frowned. "What? I like Viviana from the day I met her. She was good for you, honey. Actually, you two were perfect for each other. She gave you the support and encouragement you needed, and you gave her the stability and family that she needed. I hate that things didn't work out between you two."

Hunter's mouth fell open. "Seriously, Mom? Things would've worked out fine between us had she not ran off with my stepbrother *and* married him," Hunter bit out. From day one, his mother seemed to block that part out every time she mentioned Viviana.

"I'm sorry, son." Diana placed her hand on his shoulder and gave it a little squeeze. "I know Viviana is a touchy subject, but in light of the fact that you two own a business together, you're going to have to make peace. I hate the way things ended between you, her and Thomas. To this day, I still believe that more was at play with Viviana than what you were told."

"Well, that's one thing we agree on," Hunter mumbled and drank half the glass of lemonade.

He'd always known there had to be a good reason for why Viviana left, but his pride wouldn't allow him to dig into the situation.

She knew there wasn't anything she could ask of him that he wouldn't do. He loved her that much. They could and had talked about everything. They were best friends. Yet, she dropped him like it was the easiest thing in the world to do. No face-to-face. No conversation. Nothing. She'd made her choice, and he had moved on.

His mother's mention of Viviana's family reminded Hunter of something Thomas had said in his letter.

Oh, and good luck with that trifling mother of hers. I wouldn't be surprised if after seven years, Chandra starts showing her face again.

Hunter had no clue what that meant. No matter how trifling or manipulative Viviana's mother was, Viviana continued to let the woman walk all over her. They were the only family that each other had, and her mother used that fact to her benefit. Chandra was scandalous, and it had become a bone of contention between Viviana and Hunter. He had only tolerated the woman because of his love for her daughter. Was Thomas saying that Chandra was no longer in Viviana's life?

No way. That couldn't be the case.

"Oh, before I forget, Malik said they'll be here early tomorrow," Diane said, again snapping Hunter out of his thoughts. "Everyone else will be here in a few days. I think he said Friday. Anyway, between now and then, I want you to talk to Viviana, make peace, then invite her over this weekend."

Hunter looked at his mother to see if she was serious. She was.

He shook his head. "I might eventually make peace—maybe—but there is no way I'm inviting her over here and neither are you."

His mother sighed and stood. "Fine. If you want to go on living life wondering why she married Thomas, that's your prerogative. But if you quit being pigheaded and talk to her, maybe you can find out what really happened all those years ago." She headed out of the room, but he heard her mumble, "You got that damn stubbornness from your father's side of the family."

Hunter grunted. Maybe he had, but that still didn't change the fact that he wanted nothing to do with Viviana. So what if he never learned the reason why she had married Thomas?

He no longer cared. He had moved on.

At least that's what he was telling himself.

Chapter Six

"See, aren't you glad we decided to get out of the house?" Dannette said as the server brought them another drink.

"Yeah, I'm super excited," Viviana said dryly. She hated to admit it—but it had been a good idea to go out for drinks. She had no intentions of saying that out loud, though, since she didn't want to hear—*I told you so.*

For the last twenty-four hours, Viviana had been torturing herself with thoughts of Thomas's letter to her, owning the casino, and—more than anything—Hunter. She still couldn't believe that she'd seen him face-to-face. Knowing his relationship, or lack thereof, with Thomas, she had no reason to think that he'd been included in her late husband's will.

But he had been, and he hadn't said a word to her.

Viviana slammed back the shot of tequila, hoping it could dull her senses. It was top shelf, and Viviana was pretty sure it was setting fire to her insides as she squinted and trembled from the burn of it going down her throat.

"God, that stuff is strong," Viviana said, reaching for her

water, hoping to neutralize the liquor a little so that she didn't get drunk.

They were at what some people would refer to as a cigar bar. Some would call it a speakeasy of sorts. Viviana wasn't even sure if the place had an actual name because it was a secret establishment, exclusive private membership, frequented by elite clientele. The only way a nonmember could gain access was if a member gave them a secret code and vouched for them. Even then, access wasn't always guaranteed.

Viviana loved the exclusiveness and the relaxed vibe of the place. She liked it even more now that she didn't have to be there with Thomas.

Thinking about him immediately made her think of Hunter.

Thomas had been right about one thing—Hunter would never forgive her.

Viviana had called him last night and again this morning. Still, she hadn't heard from him. Not that she expected to. He'd been done with her seven years ago when she'd chosen his brother over him.

Walter had seemed awfully sure that Hunter wouldn't let them lose the casino, but the Hunter Viviana once knew just might. She had hurt him in the worse way, and there was no coming back from that.

She laid her head back against the leather loveseat and sighed. Evelyn Champagne King's song, "Love Come Down" played through the speakers, and Viviana soaked up the chill vibe that was floating around the space. The interior of the bar might've been masculine with wood paneling and huge dark furnishings, but it was also warm and inviting.

While the space was wide open, it was divided up where small dinner tables were in one area and sofas in another. She and Dannette were camped out on a leather loveseat that faced another one with a coffee table in the middle.

It was a cozy spot and perfect for members and their guests to have conversations without the fear of being overheard. And it gave Viviana a view around the large, open space. To her far left was a long, mahogany bar with liquor bottles that practically reached the ceiling behind it. There was also an impressive humidor room in back. In front of her were rows and rows of small wooden lockers with member's name on gold-plated tags. The compartments were used for those who wanted to store their boxes of cigars instead of carrying them back and forth or other personal items.

"He barely spared me a glance yesterday," Viviana mumbled out of the blue, knowing Dannette would know who she was talking about, since that was Viviana had talked about since seeing him. "His disgust...or maybe it was anger toward me...was palpable. Even after all of these years, I feel awful for what went down between us."

Dannette knew some of Viviana's story. Before Thomas's death, she hadn't shared much, but she'd told her friend a little bit more over the last few days. Thankfully, Dannette hadn't judged her.

"I'm telling you, Hunter is going to come around," Dannette said as she speared an olive from the charcuterie board with her fork and pointed it at Viviana. "He's not going to leave that type of money on the table. Besides, he's a gambler. What could be better than actually owning your own casino for someone like that?"

True. Viviana wasn't sure if the media was accurate, but Dannette brought up a good point. Hunter wouldn't just walk away from a casino and hotel. Maybe if she showed him how much the business was worth, he would come around. Or maybe she could explain how important the establishment was to her and appeal to his sensitive side. Heck, she'd even beg if she had to. They couldn't just toss away billions of dollars. Surely, they could work together for a year. Then if he wanted to sell, she wouldn't fight him. Who knows, maybe by then she'd even find enough money to buy him out.

Viviana sighed again and reached for a cracker and piled it with salami and cheese. Hunter's gambling situation did concern her, though. For her own sanity, she tried not to pay much attention to news about him or watch many of his games though basketball was her favorite sport. She hoped the little that she'd heard about his gambling issues weren't true.

A sudden shiver skittered up Viviana's back and she shook it off, wondering what that was about. The temperature in the building hadn't changed, and...

"Well, well, well. It looks like the man of your dreams just strolled in with an equally handsome man by his side."

Her friend could only be talking about one person. There has only been one person in the world that Viviana has ever dreamed about on a consistent basis—Hunter.

"Oh great," she mumbled sarcastically, but immediately followed her friend's gaze. And yep, there he was, the man who she couldn't stop thinking about. He was with his brother—Malik Lewis—and a pretty woman who was holding Malik's hand.

But it was Hunter who had Viviana's attention. Thanks to his height and good looks, he was hard to miss. As usual, he snagged people's attention. Most appeared to be congratulating him for the win the other night, while others nodded or gave him a wave.

He was one of those people who liked the attention and normally embraced his notoriety. Not tonight. The way his sexy mouth was set in a frown and the slight scowl on his face showed he wasn't in the mood, but he was still trying to be cordial.

In all the years that Viviana and Thomas had been hanging out at the bar, she'd never seen Hunter. It wasn't as if they were there all the time, but still, she was surprised she'd never seen him there. And of course, he would show up on a night that she was trying to scrub him out of her mind, at least for a little while.

She glanced at Malik when he pulled out the chair for his lady. The former Navy SEAL, who owned a personal security company was a giant of a man and was slightly taller and definitely wider than Hunter.

Unable to help herself, Viviana's attention went back to Hunter. It was unbelievable that after so many years, and after he'd treated her like she was invisible the day before, she was still drawn to him.

How was that possible?

Her body was on fire with need and desire, and she was pretty sure it had nothing to do with the alcohol that she'd consumed. The undesirable sensation was just like it used to be when they were together. Their attraction and connection had been so intense back in the day that Viviana could always sense when he was nearby. Maybe that had been the cause of the involuntary shiver from a moment ago.

As if sensing her looking at him, Hunter lifted his head from the menu he'd been studying and stared directly at her.

Viviana sat up straighter and gulped, but she couldn't take her eyes from his. His brows lifted slightly in surprise, and for a few seconds, they held each other's gazes, just like at Walter's office. His intense, dark eyes took her breath away.

Viviana dropped her gaze and released an unsteady breath.

"Good Lord, I'm going to need another drink," she murmured as heat rushed to her face.

Dannette snickered. "Based on the scorching look that just passed between you two, I don't think a drink is going to do much good. What y'all need is a water hose to hose you two down."

Viviana rolled her eyes at her friend and focused on the appetizers on the table in front of her. She wanted so badly to look at Hunter again, but she resisted. They definitely needed to talk, but this was not the place or the time. She wanted to have all of her faculties when they finally did have a conversation.

Feeling someone to her right, Viviana glanced up just as a short man and a tall guy who looked like a bodyguard slowed near their section.

"How you doing?" the short guy asked, squinting at her. "You look awfully familiar. I'm Frankie. Have we..." His words trailed off and he snapped his fingers and smiled. "I do know you. You're Chandra Connelly's daughter," he said, as more of a statement than a question.

Unease clawed through Viviana at the mention of her mother's name.

The mother who'd made her life a living hell from the day Viviana's father died in a car accident when she was five. And the mother she had disowned seven years ago.

"Have you seen her lately?" Frankie asked.

Viviana ran her suddenly-clammy hands down her denim-covered thighs, trying not to fidget. Normally, she didn't rattle easily, but when someone asked about her long-lost mother, Viviana couldn't help but become leery.

"I have not," she said. "We don't talk, and I haven't seen her in years."

Immediately, parts of Thomas's letter came to mind. *I won't be around to protect you...* She'd wondered what that meant at the time, and she wondered if this was someone she should be concerned about.

The man nodded slowly as his gaze slid over her before returning to her eyes. "Well, if you ever see her, tell her Frankie asked about her. Have her call me. She knows how to find me."

"I'm sure I won't be seeing her," Viviana said with more bravado than she felt.

Frankie nodded and spared Dannette a glance before returning his attention to Viviana. Then he shrugged. "Well, maybe I'll run into her while I'm in town."

Dannette pounced the moment he walked away. "Do you know who that is?" she whispered only loud enough for Viviana to hear.

"No. Should I?" she asked, finally feeling like she could breathe.

"He's a well-known, no-nonsense bookie. He splits his time between here and California, and I'm surprised you've never heard of him."

Viviana lifted an eyebrow. "And I'm surprised you have."

Dannette snorted. "I work for the owner of a casino. It's my job to know the high rollers and the lowlifes that lurk around the streets of Vegas."

Viviana narrowed her eyes at her friend. "You don't get out any more than I do. I can't believe you know people like him."

Dannette shrugged. "I hear and see things. That's why I'm so good at my job."

Viviana couldn't disagree with that, and she couldn't ask for a better assistant.

"How do you think he knows your mother? You've never mentioned her." Dannette nibbled on her lower lip in deep thought. "And how'd he know you were her daughter, especially when you don't know him?"

Those were good questions that Viviana wasn't ready to

learn the answers to, but she knew her mother. Chandra Connelly was no stranger to the gambling scene or trouble, and wherever she was hiding,

Viviana hoped she stayed there.

That was, assuming she was still alive.

Chapter Seven

Hunter stiffened the moment Frankie approached Viviana, and all of his protective instincts went on high alert. He might not want anything to do with her, but he didn't like the idea of Frankie anywhere near her. Where Hunter was sitting, he'd been able to watch their interaction without being obvious about it, and it had taken Herculean strength not to go over and get rid of him. At least the conversation hadn't lasted long—but long enough for him to tell that Viviana was uncomfortable.

Did they know each other?

Or was Frankie hitting on her?

There were plenty of women there...why Viviana?

Questions bombarded Hunter, but there was one thing he knew for sure even if he hadn't seen her in years—she and Frankie didn't travel in the same circle. That, he'd bet money on.

No doubt Viviana was still what he and some of his buddies called a good girl. There was no way in hell that she'd associate with someone like the bookie. The fact that she was in a bar was even a surprise to him. She hadn't been much of a drinker when they were together, and he couldn't imagine that she'd changed that much.

Then again, that had been a long time ago, he reminded himself. The woman he once knew also wouldn't have married his stepbrother.

Yet, she had.

"Hunter?" Malik said, kicking him under the table.

Hunter startled and glanced at his brother. "What?" But then he noticed the server standing next to the table. "I'm sorry, you say something?"

"I was asking if I can get you anything from the bar while you review the menu," the woman said.

"Yeah, let me have a Blanton's Straight from the Barrel," he said. Many places didn't carry that bourbon, but this wasn't just any place. All of their alcohol was top-shelf and, in some cases, very hard to find.

Hunter returned his attention to the menu. He hadn't been there in months, and he was glad to see they still had one of his favorites—steak burger and onion rings.

"Actually, can we go ahead and order our food, too?"

Thankfully, his brother and sister-in-law knew what they wanted, and they all placed their order before the server walked away.

"You being distracted wouldn't have anything to do with your ex sitting across the room, would it?" Malik asked.

His eagle-eyed brother, who was ten years older, was the most observant person Hunter knew. Even when it didn't look like Malik was checking out his surroundings, he was. He probably knew where all of the exits were, who was caring a concealed weapon, and how many people were in the building. The guy didn't miss anything.

"I'm surprised you remember what she looks like," Hunter

said, gazing in Viviana's direction again. It appeared Frankie had left the building, but there was no way he'd leave without saying something to Hunter. He'd want to make sure that he was seen and that the message was clear—Hunter could leave LA, but Frankie could find him anywhere if he wanted to.

"Of course, I remember her. She's the only woman who's ever caught your attention and held it."

"Yeah, until she didn't," Hunter mumbled, sounding as bitter as he felt. He was still on edge, but his attitude had improved a little from the day before. So that was progress.

"Okay, what am I missing here?" Natasha, Hunter's sister-in-law asked, glancing from him to her husband and back again.

Malik set his menu down and put his arm around his wife before pulling her close. "Viviana's here, and my brother can't stop looking at her."

Hunter didn't bother denying it, because it was true. Every few minutes, his gaze just went in the direction where she was sitting. And almost every time, she was looking at him, too.

Natasha gasped. "Really? Where?" She started to turn, but Malik stopped her and nodded toward a large mirror that was hanging on the wall behind Hunter.

"She's behind us to the left with short hair and dark skin, sitting with another woman," Malik described.

"Oh, she's beautiful, Hunter," Natasha said loud enough to be heard over the music, but not loud enough for others nearby to hear. "No wonder you freaked out over seeing her again."

"Clearly having good taste in women runs in the family," Malik said, and kissed his wife.

Hunter had to agree with her opinion of Viviana and with what his brother said. Viviana was as gorgeous as she'd been the first time he met her years ago.

As for Natasha, the chief of staff at one of Chicago's largest hospitals, she was as beautiful as she was smart. Tall and curvy, she had long, brownish-red hair that hung over her shoulders and complemented her light-toffee complexion. Her African-American and Hispanic heritage was evident in her facial features, as well as the subtle accent that snuck through when she said certain words.

She was the best thing to ever happen to his brother, and Hunter had never seen Malik happier. They'd been married five years and had two really cool kids—a four-year-old daughter and a three-year-old son. He wasn't sure if they planned to have more, but Hunter wouldn't mind having a few more nieces and nephews to spoil.

Malik and Natasha knew about Thomas's will, the hotel and casino, and thanks to his mother, they also knew he wanted nothing to do with Viviana. Neither one judged him, but he could tell that Natasha had been in agreement with his mother. He needed to make peace with Viviana and claim his inheritance.

The server returned with their drinks, and a few minutes later, their meals were delivered. Hunter hadn't seen the whole family in over six months, not since the Christmas holiday, and even then, it hadn't been a long visit. His games schedule was grueling during the season and traveling for pleasure was limited. He had gotten a chance to hang out with Malik a weekend in February when his brother met him at the All-Star game. That was always a good time.

For the next few minutes, they chatted over their meal, and Hunter felt better than he'd felt in a couple of days. The situation between him, Viviana, and Thomas were still at the forefront of his mind, but at least it wasn't stressing him out as much.

Hunter glanced up when the server returned with another drink for him. "Umm, I didn't order another one." He glanced at Malik to see if maybe he had ordered it, but his brother shook his head.

"Actually, it came from one of the women over there." She nodded to where Viviana and her friend had been sitting. Now they were standing, gathering their bags and heading for the front exit.

If Hunter was going to talk to her, now would be the time, but he didn't move. He wasn't ready. Maybe in the morning he'd at least return her calls.

"Thank you," he said to the server.

Seconds after she strolled away, Hunter had another visitor stop by his table.

"Hunter Graham. So we meet again."

Hunter sighed at the sight of Frankie. This time Keith wasn't with him, but there was no doubt that he was nearby. Frankie didn't travel alone. It would be too dangerous.

"What's up, Frankie? Surprised to see you here in Vegas," Hunter said before taking a sip of his drink.

His nonchalant attitude was probably driving Frankie nuts, but Hunter didn't care. He liked seeing the man stew. No doubt he was frustrated even though he knew that Hunter was capable of paying and would...in his own time. He would not be bullied.

"Sorry to interrupt your meal," Frankie said, sounding genuinely sorry as he spoke to Malik and Natasha, then turned to Hunter. "Can I holler at you for a minute?"

"Sure." Hunter took a healthy swig of his drink before standing. He hated to look at his brother, already knowing he was going to see an inquiring expression on his face. The good thing about having his brother there, though, was that if Frankie and his goon decided to take things too far, Malik would have his back.

"Be back in a sec," Hunter said, and followed Frankie to the rear of the building.

When they reached the end of a long hallway, Hunter spotted Keith near the door to the Bugsy room—named after the mobster—Bugsy Siegel.

Keith pushed open the door and they all walked into the empty space. The room was only used if the front of the establishment was full, which it wasn't at the moment. The space was a smaller version of what was out front, except it included a poker table as well as a pool table.

The moment the door was closed, Keith grabbed Hunter's upper arm and shoved him further into the room.

"Man, get the hell off of me." Hunter jerked out of the man's hold and pushed him back. "Frankie, I suggest you call off your watchdog, because if he ever puts his hands on me again, you're going to need to hire new help."

"So, you thought you could just leave town to get away from me? Surely, you know me better than that. I have eyes everywhere, and I know what you're planning before you even do it. You got my money?"

"Dude, I'm on vacation. I didn't expect to see you here. So no, I don't have your money on me. I'll get it to you in a couple of weeks—and don't worry, it will include the full amount plus interest. Why you sweating me like this? You know I'm good for it. Yet, you're treating me like one of your lowlife customers who can't pay."

Out of nowhere, Keith punched him in the gut, and Hunter gasped, then doubled over trying to catch his breath. He eventually stood upright and glared at Keith. "So that's how you operate? You sucker-punch people?

Without thinking, Hunter lunged forward and grabbed Keith around the waist, tackling him to the floor. The man might've been strong, but Hunter had frustration on his side as he punched the guy. He started to hit him again, and Keith landed his fist into Hunter's jaw, but Hunter still had him pinned to the floor. Growing up wrestling with Malik had paid off.

Breathing hard, Hunter was just about to hit Keith again when he heard a gun cock and felt cold metal against the back of his head.

"You've caused me more trouble than it's worth." Frankie's gravelly voice sounded close to Hunter's ear. "Maybe I should just put a bullet in your head and be done with this shit. All I want is my money, but you're acting like you're untouchable or something. Hell, I should be the one asking you what's up with that. What are you, broke or something? Is that why you're stalling in paying me what you owe?"

"Man, even if I never played ball again, I wouldn't be broke. I got the money. I just don't appreciate you trying to tell me what I'm going to do and when I have to do it. I'll pay you when I pay you."

Frankie released a humorless laugh. "You're talking pretty tough for a man who has a gun at your head."

"And you don't know who you're dealing with if you think I won't put a bullet in you and your helper."

Hunter groaned when he heard the lethalness in Malik's voice. His brother was crazy enough to follow through with the threat. Especially since he was a fight-first-and-ask-questions-later kind of guy.

"Set the gun down slowly," Malik instructed, and Frankie obeyed. "Now, stand up. Both of you."

When Frankie backed off, Hunter moved away from Keith and they both scurried to their feet.

Hunter was shocked to see Malik holding two guns, one on each guy. His brother was a giant of a man and a few inches taller than Hunter. A former Navy SEAL, as well as a weapons specialist, *fearless* was the man's middle name. There was no doubt he could take these guys on without breaking a sweat. He might've looked professional in his button-down shirt, dress pants, and wearing a pair of Stacy Adams shoes, but deep down, he was deadlier than a Mafia king.

"Now get out," Malik growled, nodding his head back toward the door.

Frankie glanced at the floor where his gun was laying.

"You won't be needing that," Malik said. "And just so you know, the moment you put a gun to my brother's head was the moment you made an enemy for life. Now...get the fuck out of here."

Frankie glared at Hunter. "You sure this is how you want this to go down?" he asked, his voice rumbling with anger. "Because if I walk out of this room without my weapon and what you owe me, we're done."

And by *done*, Hunter knew the bookie meant that if Hunter didn't pay up immediately, not only wouldn't he be accepting future bets from him, but he was coming for his money. Hunter also knew that the man's bark was worse than his bite. Still, he wasn't planning to have any dealings with Frankie in the future.

"Like I've told you several times, I have your money," Hunter said. "I'll be in touch soon." *When I'm damn good and ready*, he wanted to add, but kept that thought to himself.

The rage showing on the little man's face would've made a weaker man shake in his boots, but Hunter wasn't worried. No way was the guy stupid enough to come after him. Frankie knew better. He didn't want the type of heat or attention that coming after Hunter would bring.

When they walked out, Hunter whirled on his brother. "Dude, I was handling it. Why did you step in? I'm not a kid. I don't need you fighting my battles. They're gonna think I'm some type of punk."

Malik shoved one of his guns into his back waistband and the other in a holster at his ankle. He glanced around the room until he spotted a cloth napkin. Grabbing it, he carefully picked up Frankie's weapon and wrapped it in the napkin.

"So, you're such a badass that you let those motherfuckers get the jump on you," he finally spoke. "From where I was standing, you were getting your ass kicked and was about to get your fuckin' head blown off."

"Does Tasha know you still have a cursing problem?" Hunter asked, trying to deflect. He had never known a person whose every other word was a curse word. After Malik had gotten married, his language had gotten better...except when Tasha wasn't around.

"Seriously, man. I was handling it. You didn't have to go all gangster on them."

"Your egotistical ass is going to get yourself killed, but not on my watch. Mom would've strangled me if you ended up in a body bag tonight. As for them thinking you're a punk? You are *—my punk-ass little brother.*"

Hunter couldn't help but laugh. That was how Malik used to introduce him when they were growing up. At ten years older than Hunter, he was tasked with letting Hunter follow him and his buddies around.

"So, what was that shit all about, anyway?" Malik asked, folding his arms across his chest while still holding Frankie's gun in one hand. "How much do you owe, and why haven't you paid them?"

"Never mind what I owe. I don't take kindly to people trying to bully me into doing anything. Of course, I have the money, and I'll pay Frankie when I'm good and ready. He just wanted to remind me who I was dealing with, and this is me letting him know who he's dealing with."

Malik shook his head and sighed loudly. "Quit being an asshole and pay the man. The next time you might not be so lucky." He walked to the door, but stopped and turned to Hunter. "Oh, and if your gambling issues get any worse, and somehow puts Mom in danger, I'm gonna kill your mother-fuckin' ass myself."

Hunter watched Malik stalk out of the room, knowing his brother was dead serious.

Chapter Eight

Viviana had just gotten off the phone from another call when her desk phone buzzed.

"Ugh!" she growled. "Give me a break."

Her morning had been full of meetings and one call after another. If this was any indication of how the rest of the day was going, she might quit.

"No. I'm not quitting," she said into the quietness of her office. She couldn't quit. There were too many people counting on her to get it all right. And that's exactly what she planned to do.

Her phone buzzed again, and this time she answered. "Yes, Dannette?"

"Ms. Connelly, you have a visitor," her assistant said.

It must've been someone important who didn't work for the company. Dannette never called her Ms. Connelly.

Viviana had her finger over the intercom button, prepared to respond, but then Dannette said, "Mr. Hunter Graham is here to see you."

Viviana froze. What was he doing there? Sure, she had

called him several times yesterday, before seeing him at the bar, and again this morning. She had only expected a call back, not an in-person visit.

"Okay, be cool," she told herself then glanced down at her outfit. She was wearing a yellow, sleeveless dress with a V-neck that was low enough to be a little sexy, but not too low. The garment hugged her body and showed off her trim waist and how hard she worked out at the gym every day. There was a jacket that went with the outfit, but it was hanging on the back of her chair. Maybe she should slip it on. Would that make her look more professional?

No. I look fine. I just need to...

"Shall I send him in?" Dannette asked.

Oh, crap. Viviana forgot she hadn't responded. She pressed the button. "Let me finish up...actually, give me two minutes."

She made a mad dash to the attached bathroom where she kept an extra makeup bag. Glancing in the mirror, Viviana ran her fingers through her short curls.

She had cut her hair and had gone natural a few years ago after Thomas told her he liked her hair long and straight. He hadn't thought her natural curls looked professional enough, but she showed him. Going against his wishes had been a bold move, but she'd done it. He hadn't said much. Yet, the disapproving expression that had been written on his face had said it all.

An easy smile kicked up the corners of her mouth.

I'm free. She could do whatever the hell she wanted, and it felt so damn good.

As Viviana studied herself in the mirror, she grabbed a tube of lipstick and noticed how happier she looked. The years with Thomas had felt like a lifetime of unhappiness, and going forward, she planned to live her life to the fullest. Bold and courageous. That's who she was, and now it was time to show that side of herself.

Viviana gave herself one last look and put everything away before returning to her office, and just in time. A knock sounded on the door seconds before it swung open.

Where she was standing, slightly out of sight, her visitor couldn't see her without stepping further into the office. That's when Dannette appeared, her gaze sweeping the room before landing on Viviana.

"Hey," she said, giving Viviana a quick once-over before smiling her approval. "I have Mr. Graham with me."

She turned back and motioned for him to enter, and Viviana braced herself.

Would her body respond the same way it had the other day at the attorney's office? Or had that just been shock?

I guess I'll find out.

When Hunter's large frame came into view, his presence sucked all the air out of the room. He was a giant of a man, but it wasn't just his height and size that commanded attention. It was everything about him. From his handsome face to his confidence, which was borderline arrogance, he used to own whatever space he was in.

That hadn't changed.

Viviana didn't know how long they stood there, staring at each other. The man was so damn handsome, it hurt to look at him. He was dressed in a two-piece white linen outfit that made him look like African royalty.

And just like the other day, the moment was so surreal. It was as if he came out of nowhere and stepped into one of her dreams—and she'd had many. Now that he was there in real life, she wasn't sure what to say.

"Hello, Viviana," he said before she could open her mouth,

and his deep voice swirled around her like a gentle breeze kissing her heated skin.

Oh, boy. How was she going to hold an intelligent conversation when her words wouldn't come? Stunned into silence was clearly a thing, because she was stuck in place with jumbled thoughts and only the sound of her pulse pounding in her ear.

Say something! she told herself. Still...nothing.

Someone cleared their throat, and Viviana startled. She hadn't realized Dannette was still standing there, grinning like an idiot. But seeing her was enough to snap Viviana out of whatever trance she'd been in. Thankfully, her friend was standing slightly behind Hunter, and he couldn't see her comical facial expression.

"Thanks, Dannette. That'll be all," Viviana managed to say.

Still smiling, her friend gave her a slight bow and backed out of the office.

As soon as the door was closed, Viviana finally spoke to Hunter. "What are you doing here?" The words flew from her mouth before she organized them in her head. "I mean...I didn't expect you to show up."

"I figured it was time I start acting like I'm part owner of a hotel and casino. Sorry it took me so long to get my shit together. May I?" he said, nodding toward the chairs in front of the desk.

"Of course. I'm sorry. Please forgive me. You just caught me off guard," she said in a rush and reclaimed her desk chair while he sat in one of the visitor's seats.

"Yeah, I know that feeling," he mumbled. He sat back and leaned his arm on the chair next to him, looking relaxed and in control. While she, on the other hand, was trembling inside.

Relax, she told herself. *He's just a man...he's just a smoking hot, good-looking man who I haven't seen up close and personal in, like, forever.*

"You look good," she blurted, and heat spread through her body like a wildfire, threatening to burn her alive. She hadn't planned to share her thoughts out loud. "I mean..."

A roguish grin spread across his lips, and Viviana was pretty sure she groaned out loud. *God, help me.* She didn't want to make a total fool of herself during their first real interaction. It was time to get herself together.

She sat up straighter and pulled her shoulders back. She oversaw a billion-dollar business with thousands of staff members. There was no reason for her to be nervous.

He's just a man, she reminded herself.

But that wasn't true. Hunter was so much more. He was the man she had vowed to love and support. The man she'd planned to raise a family with. And the man she had wanted to spend the rest of her life with...until she'd had to walk away.

Viviana dropped her gaze to the desk as guilt slashed through her. How were they ever going to work together? There was no way he'd ever be able to forgive her. Heck, she had yet to forgive herself.

If there was a way to turn back time and have a do-over, she would handle things very differently. At the time, she didn't think she had any other choice but to marry Thomas. Now she was older, wiser, and knew better. But it was too late. She had lost Hunter forever, and that was the biggest regret of her life.

"I know you don't want to be here," she said, unable to keep the defeat out of her tone. "But, Hunter, thank you for coming. This is hard for me—seeing you again. So, I know it can't be easy for you."

He didn't respond, so she continued.

"There's something I've wanted to say to you for years, but I knew you wouldn't want to hear it." She inhaled deeply and released the breath slowly as she got her nerves under control. "I'm sorry. I am so sorry I hurt you. I know it's too late and it doesn't mean anything to you, but I really am sorry."

Still, he said nothing, but after a few seconds of studying her, he finally said, "I forgive you."

It was a good thing she was sitting, because Viviana felt as if she was going to faint. Though she meant every word of her apology, she never expected to hear him say—*I forgive you.*

It was as if a weight had been lifted from her shoulders and emotion swelled inside of her. *He forgives me.* She blinked rapidly trying to keep the sudden tears at bay as her mind processed what that meant. Those three simple words were powerful enough to turn the darkest day into sunshine, and she soaked them up.

It was still early, though. He could just be saying it and not really mean it. But she was going to take it because they had to figure out a way to work together. Time would tell if he really did forgive her.

"Thank you. That means more than you'll ever know," she choked out, then cleared her throat. "I assume Walter talked to you about the stipulations in the will?"

Hunter nodded. "Yeah. He suggested that I stick it out for a year. Otherwise, neither of us would get a dime, and the company would go to some financial group."

Viviana nodded. "Yeah, it was how Thomas had written it up. I don't know what type of game he's playing, but I've worked my ass off to make this casino into what it is today."

"That's what Walter said. You have a fan in him, by the way. He spoke very highly of you and said that you deserved the casino *and* the hotel."

Viviana frowned. "He said that?"

Granted, he knew about the marriage contract, but she thought he was just another one of Thomas's lackeys doing his bidding. But now that she thought about the reading of the will, and how kind he'd been during it and even times before, maybe he'd been an ally of hers all along.

Hunter nodded. "It's nice to see that you put your business degree to work. I don't know how you ended up with Thomas, and I don't want to know," he said quickly. "But I am curious— why do you think he left the business to both of us? He hated me, and based on something Walter let slip, I have a feeling that things weren't all that great between you and my step-brother. So why leave us the casino and the hotel?"

Viviana snorted, but quickly covered her mouth with her hand. "Oops, sorry. I was around your brother for the last seven years, and I didn't understand half the things he did or why. I honestly didn't expect him to leave me anything. He wasn't..." She stopped herself from continuing, hating that she'd said that much.

"Why didn't you think he'd leave you anything?" Hunter asked.

Viviana debated on what to say. Hunter had already made it clear that he didn't want to know why she ended up with Thomas. What could she say without saying too much?

She sighed and toyed with the edge of a file folder that was sitting on her desk. "Thomas and I didn't have the type of rela-tionship you might think we had. He...he wasn't a nice guy."

Hunter knew his brother well enough to know that he was a narcissistic jerk.

What he didn't know was that sometimes his brother exhib-ited Jekyll-and-Hyde behavior. Which was just her opinion.

Instead of sharing that, she said, "I have no idea why he did half the things he did. Or why he left the business to us. At first, I was leery, expecting it to be some type of cruel trick, but Walter assured me the casino and the hotel are ours as long as we don't sell it within the year. With that said, I'll be happy to share any and everything about the organization with you. Just let me know what your schedule looks like, and we can set up some time to meet."

Viviana wasn't sure how she'd be able to spend any amount of time with him and not long for more. She would never admit it out loud, but she missed him so much she physically ached. Those months after leaving him, she'd fallen into a deep depression.

It wasn't until Thomas hired her on at the casino that she started to pull herself up out of the abyss of despair. Still, not a day went by that she didn't think of Hunter...that she didn't long to be in his strong arms again.

Now here he was...forgiving her and giving her hope that they could move on from there.

And for the sake of the business and their partnership, she had to try to keep a level head and not do something stupid. Like fall into his arms and beg for a second chance.

A knock sounded on the door, and Viviana told whoever it was to come in.

"Sorry to bother you, but there's a delivery for Mr. Graham." Dannette held up a large white bag and a small, brown paper bag.

Hunter stood. "Thanks. I ordered us lunch before I came. Oh, and Dannette, call me Hunter. You'll be seeing me around. We might as well get on a first-name basis." He turned to Viviana. "Unless there's a rule in place that everyone has to be addressed by Mr. or Miss."

Viviana shook her head. "No, unless that's a change you'd want to make. Since you are one of the owners now."

She said that last part with a smile- and he returned it.

"Cool. I think being on a first-name basis works. Now, how about some lunch?"

Dannette still had that goofy grin on her face as she quietly eased out of the room, closing the door behind her. No doubt she would hound Viviana for all the details later.

"I hope you still like lobster rolls. I ordered some from a restaurant inside of the Venetian. If you haven't tried them, they are the best. I also ordered you extra butter."

Viviana sat, stunned that he remembered her favorite meal. Her heart swelled, and she feared it would pop right out of her chest. Maybe he really had forgiven her.

"Thank you," she managed to say around the lump in her throat. "I haven't had a lobster roll in seven years." She hadn't planned to volunteer that last bit of information, but it was true. There was no way she'd be able to eat one without thinking of Hunter, so she hadn't.

As a matter of fact, there'd been a lot of things she had stopped doing for the same reason.

Hunter stood silently in front of the desk, staring at her in surprise, but he didn't question her.

Thank goodness.

She was a little embarrassed by the admission, but a small part of her was glad he knew. She wanted more than anything to tell him that she'd missed him like crazy and that her life had felt like nothing without him in it. But she didn't say any of that. What would be the point? They could never be a couple again, and she would do good to remember that.

"I guess it's well overdue for you to have one of your favorite meals again," he finally said and started pulling items out of the bag. He set the food up on her desk, and a sweet thrill charged through her body.

I'm free.

She and Hunter might just be able to get through this next year in peace after all.

At least Viviana hoped.

Chapter Nine

Hunter was glad he had come to see Viviana. The visit was going better than he expected. He thought he'd feel some of the anguish that he'd felt years ago, or even what he'd been experiencing the last couple of days where she was concerned.

He didn't.

Emotionally, it was a little unnerving being near her again, but physically, it was another story. His attraction to her was as strong as it had been years ago when they were a couple.

The moment he had entered her office and saw her standing there, his dick had leaped to attention. It didn't give a damn that she was off-limits. It was that look that she'd given him when their gazes connected. He hadn't seen that expression in a long time and it stirred up memories of them having wild, passionate sex. He'd wanted to charge across the room and take her hard and fast up against the nearest wall.

No surprise there. No one had ever come close to making him lose control the way Viviana used to do. She always made him feel powerful, needed, and desired. Like he was the most important person in the world. Then it all came to an end.

Hunter studied her now across the desk while she ate, and took note of how stunning she was in the yellow dress. The color was beautiful against her dark skin, and it was nice to see that she still favored bright colors. His gaze traveled lower, over her long graceful neck and down to her full tempting breasts. They might've been hidden by the lightweight garment, but he remembered what lay beneath the material.

Hell, he remembered everything about her luscious body and what it took to make her come for him.

Dammit. He had to stop.

He looked away, not liking the route his brain was taking him. They couldn't go back to the way things used to be. They were two different people, and this was a different day and time. Too much had happened, things that might've been forgivable, but not forgettable.

"Mmm, oh, my goodness, this is so good," Viviana said as she bit into the lobster roll. "This one might be the best I ever had. *God,* Hunter..."

She moaned again, and Hunter was tempted to snatch the sandwich out of her hands.

Damn her. She was killing him.

The worst part was that she didn't have a clue about how much she was turning him on. He had temporarily forgotten about the erotic sounds she made when she was eating something she loved. It was damn near orgasmic.

The moaning, groaning, and the little shimmy she was doing in her seat, it was as if she'd forgotten that he was sitting across from her. It would've been comical if her ass wasn't turning him on even more.

He couldn't take it. The woman was wreaking havoc on his peace of mind.

"Mmm," she moaned again with her eyes closed, and Hunter must've made a sound or something because suddenly her eyes popped open. She straightened in her seat and set the sandwich down. This time he did chuckle at her sheepish expression.

"Sorry," she said. "I—I don't know what came over me. It's just that it's been so long since I've enjoyed anything as much as I have this lobster roll."

He wondered what else she'd gone without since leaving him.

No. No. I don't want to know, he told himself. It's best if they discussed business before the conversation went in the wrong direction. That would include any discussion about her life with Thomas.

"Thomas and I didn't have the type of relationship you might think we had. He...he wasn't a nice guy."

Her words from earlier entered his mind. Exactly what the hell type of relationship had they had? He wanted to know... then again, he didn't. It had been hard enough for him to stop by her office and call a truce. Having to hear about her marriage to his stepbrother would be too much...at least right now.

"Oh, shoot. I knew I was forgetting something," Viviana said, and stood abruptly. "Excuse me for a second."

Hunter finished off his sandwich and tossed the wrapper and napkins into a nearby trash can. He sat back in his seat and folded his arms across his chest.

While he waited, he thought about the conversation he'd had with Malik earlier after they'd played basketball. The house that Hunter was renting had an impressive indoor court and playing a little one-on-one had relaxed him some.

Malik brought up the subject of Frankie and gambling. By the time the discussion was over, Hunter knew he needed to quit screwing around with the bookie. Not that he was afraid of the guy—he wasn't—but Hunter had too many other things happening in his life right now.

He paid Frankie what he owed plus interest. Instead of going to see the man personally, he had the money delivered.

Now Hunter could move on from the bookie and focus on more important aspects of his life. Besides being one of the new owners of TGR Grand Hotel and Casino—a name he planned to change in the near future—he had the media to watch out for. They knew about his inheritance and were once again trying to paint his love for gambling as an addiction rather than a hobby. He didn't have an addiction, but trying to convince them and the NBA to believe that was going to be even harder.

The day before he flew to Las Vegas, he'd had to meet with the owners of his team. It had been a mandatory meeting. Hunter hadn't been surprised when they'd voiced their concerns about how much he and his gambling issue had been in the news lately. One of the owners and the basketball commissioner felt a need to remind him that he was making the league look bad.

Apparently, winning the national championship didn't mean much—which was why he was seriously thinking about retiring after this next season. Even more so now after receiving the inheritance.

"Okay, sorry about that," Viviana said when she reentered the office and reclaimed her seat. "Now that I've taken care of a few things, do you want to talk about TGR Grand?"

"Sure, and in the near future, I'd like for us to consider changing the name," Hunter said and draped his arm on the back of the chair to make himself more comfortable.

He didn't miss the way Viviana's eyes followed his every move. Nor did he miss the way her gaze skittered over his upper body before quickly looking away.

Good. I'm not the only one affected.

"Name change? You'll get no argument from me," she said and pulled several folders from one of the drawers in her desk. "Let me tell you a little about the company."

Viviana talked about the casino and what she did on a daily basis. It was clear that she loved her job even if she was overseeing several departments. Despite the fact he spent a lot of time in casinos, Hunter had no clue what all went into running them. There were over six thousand employees working at the casino alone, and just as many who worked at the hotel. He hadn't even realized that the two were operated as separate entities.

"As you learn more about the operations, you can let me know what role you want to play. Oh, and that reminds me, I've set up a mandatory management meeting for tomorrow morning. I hope you're able to attend. I want you to meet some key players in the organization, especially Xavier Black. He's the VP of Operations for the hotel."

Hunter nodded. "I can be here."

They talked a while longer, and Hunter's brain was spinning. He didn't know the first thing about running an organization, but Viviana had him excited about learning. The timing of everything was perfect since he'd been thinking about retiring from the league soon. This unexpected change in his life would give him an opportunity to put his degree in communications to good use.

"Unfortunately, with my basketball schedule, I'm not sure how much help I'll be. I definitely want to play an active role here, but remember, I pretty much travel most of the year."

"I'm sure we'll figure something out," Viviana said.

Hunter glanced at his watch. "I didn't realize it was getting so late. I need to get going, but I'll make sure I'm here for the meeting tomorrow."

"Great. Oh, before you go, we should probably exchange contact information."

"Is this you trying to get my phone number?" he cracked, and almost laughed at how flustered she suddenly seemed. He was pretty sure if her skin wasn't so dark that he'd see a blush painting her cheeks.

"I—I wasn't..."

Hunter chuckled. "I'm messing with you, Vivi. Of course we should exchange information." The nickname he used to call her surprisingly rolled off his tongue with ease. That was a good sign that he was feeling comfortable around her.

The next few months should be interesting.

Who knows, maybe one day we can be more than business partners...

The thought screeched to a halt. He was getting way ahead of himself. No way was he going to let her get close to his heart again. He couldn't handle her crushing it a second time. But he'd be lying if he said that he wasn't interested in getting to know her again.

Tread lightly, dude. Tread lightly...

Chapter Ten

The moment Hunter left her office, Viviana dropped back against her seat and released a relieved breath. Their impromptu meeting had gone extremely well, leaving her hopeful about their new partnership.

Thomas might've been trying to bring them together to cause more pain—which it did, in a sense—but his meddling could have a different effect. Her reunion with Hunter could be the best thing to happen to her in a long time.

A smile broke out on her face when she thought about the lobster roll. How embarrassing to let him see how much she'd enjoyed it. God, it was so good. She was definitely going to have to find out where in the Venetian hotel he'd gotten it. Maybe she'd pick up another one for dinner.

Dannette burst into the office. "Okay, I want to know *everything*, but first, Xavier stopped by to see you. He wants you to call him as soon as you're free."

"Actually, I need to stretch my legs. I'll go down and see him." All of the management offices for both the casino and hotel were housed in the casino's building. They occupied the top two floors, which made it convenient for meeting.

Viviana stood and pulled out the bottom drawer that contained her handbag. She grabbed her cell phone and keys.

"As for the meeting with Hunter, I'll fill you in tonight over dinner."

"Yes! I can't wait. I'll supply the wine, and can I just say, that man is even more beautiful in real life. I can't believe you walked away from all of that deliciousness," she said, and ran out of the office when her desk phone started ringing.

A stab of guilt slammed into Viviana. There was so much Dannette didn't know, and Viviana didn't think she'd ever share her full story with anyone. Except for maybe Hunter. If ever he wanted to know the whole ugly truth, she'd tell him.

He deserved that much.

She left her office and passed Dannette, who was still on the phone. If only her friend knew that walking away from Hunter had almost killed her. It had been the hardest thing in the world to do, and Viviana would never wish that type of emotional pain on even her worst enemy.

I'm lucky Hunter forgave me.

If he hadn't, there was probably no way they could run a business together. As it was, seeing him more often was going to be crazy hard, but Viviana was looking forward to spending time with him. She had no false expectations that there could ever be anything more than a partnership.

Yet, there'd been a moment this afternoon that she thought...*what if?*

What if they got along great and rekindled their friendship?

Or what if they put the past behind them and started fresh with more than friendship?

It could happen...on her part. Especially since she had

never stop loving him. He was a hard man to forget...or get over, and between the heated gazes between them and the fact that he'd brought her a lobster roll...

Anything was possible.

As she strolled to the stairs, Viviana glanced at the screen of her cell phone noting that she had missed three text messages from Xavier, telling her to call him.

What was up with him? He'd been calling and texting her more and acting stranger than usual. There was one thing in Thomas's letter that she had agreed with—Xavier was a lousy manager. Mainly because of his poor communication skills. He had some good ideas from a business perspective, but they really needed someone in his role who was more of a leader.

Viviana glanced up just as she reached the door to the stairs and pushed it open.

Maybe we can get him some training. Then...

She gasped when she stepped into the stairwell, and someone grabbed her wrist. She snatched her arm back before she realized who it was.

"Christ, Xavier! You scared me. What's wrong with you sneaking up on somebody like that? And why are you hanging out in the stairwell?"

"Why have you been avoiding my calls and text messages?" he asked, ignoring her question. "The same thing happened yesterday. Why didn't you call me back?"

He moved toward her like a predator, and Viviana inched backward until she bumped into the wall. Unease clawed through her at the wildness in his eyes. She hated that they were in a confined space, and if she screamed, it was possible that no one would hear her.

"I already told you not to use my cell number for business calls," she said with more bravado than she felt at the moment, but she couldn't show fear. "If you want to talk to me about work, call my office phone. Or do like you did earlier and leave a message with my assistant."

He moved closer and she took a step to the side.

"If those were personal calls," she said quickly, "we've had this conversation months ago. I told you I wasn't comfortable with the way you were calling me, especially when you asked me out, even though I was married. Like I told you then, I'm not interested in anything but a professional relationship with you. You already disrespected me and my husband when you asked me to dinner. He might be gone, but I'm still not interested."

Xavier released a humorless laugh. "You make it sound as if you and Thomas had a real marriage. You forget, he and I have known each other for a very long time. He wasn't in love with you. He only married you to get back at his brother. Surely, you had to know that. Besides, he said that you weren't giving him any. So, it couldn't have been much of a relationship."

Anger knotted inside of her. How dare Thomas tell this asshole anything about her or their sham of a marriage? What else had he told him?

Whatever—it was enough to make Xavier think he could talk to her any way he wanted. He and Thomas had attended college together, and Thomas had hired him soon after opening the hotel.

"Let's just stop the games," Xavier said and reached out to touch her face, but Viviana leaned away from him.

When she took another sidestep, she realized she was cornered. "I'm not playing any games with you, Xavier. Now move out of my way."

"I know you're interested in me just like I'm interested in you. I've known it for months, but I don't understand why you're still playing hard to get. Now that Thomas is gone, God rest his soul, there's nothing to stand in our way. Besides, he told me months ago, the night of his birthday party, that if I could get you, I could have you."

Fury sparked inside of her. "You have clearly lost your mind if you think that just because you want me that I'll automatically be yours! It doesn't work that way. I'm not some property that Thomas could just hand off. Now back the hell up unless you want one of my high heels up your delusional ass."

She released a scream when Xavier grabbed her arm and jerked her to him. "You think you're too good for me or something?"

He jammed his mouth over hers and panic racketed inside of her as she turned her head side to side and struggled to get out of his hold. "Thomas was a fool to not demand that you fulfill your wifely duties, but maybe I should teach you—"

"What the hell are you doing?" Hunter roared and grabbed the back of Xavier's shirt, then slammed him against the wall. He punched him in the face and sent him crashing to the floor.

Xavier cried out and scrambled backward, holding his jaw as he glared at Hunter. "This...this is none of your business," he growled.

"You fucking asshole, you made it my business when you put your hands on her!" Hunter yelled and charged toward him, but Viviana grabbed on to the back of his shirt.

"Don't. He's not worth it," she said, unable to help the tremor in her voice. The last thing she wanted was for Hunter to get into any type of trouble for hurting or killing the guy.

The door to the hallway burst open, slamming against the wall and two of the casino's security stood in the doorway. "Mrs. Re—"

"Escort him off the premises and make sure he never steps foot in the hotel or the casino," Viviana said with more boldness than she felt at the moment. She couldn't seem to stop shaking, but she refused to let Xavier or Hunter see how much the attack affected her.

"You can't do this!" Xavier yelled as the two men carried him out of the stairwell. "Let me go! She came onto me, tempting me..."

Dannette and a secretary were in the doorway.

"Are you okay?" Dannette asked Viviana, worry on her face. "I called security when I heard a scream. I didn't realize—"

"I—I'm all right. I just need..." Viviana swallowed and quickly batted tears away as the realization of what Xavier could have done to her hit her.

Hunter stood in front of her, and Viviana covered her face with her hands as tears blurred her vision.

"I got her, Dannette," Hunter said.

He pulled Viviana against his tall body and wrapped his strong arms around her.

Dannette said something, but Viviana didn't hear what. Instead, she clung to Hunter and let her tears flow freely. Her sobs were muffled against his chest as he whispered comforting words.

Viviana wasn't sure how long they stood that way, but in that moment, she never wanted him to let her go.

* * *

Hours later, Hunter was still angry about the attack on Viviana. He couldn't ever remember being as angry as he'd been when he found Xavier with his hands on her. He hated hearing about men taking advantage of women, but when that woman was Viviana, he wanted to punch something.

Better yet, he wanted to punch Xavier over and over again.

Right now, they were in Viviana's office. Most of the administrative staff had gone home for the day, and all of them were shocked to hear the news about Xavier. He had since been arrested and would probably get charged with aggravated assault.

At least Viviana wouldn't have to worry about him again. She wasn't his first victim.

A woman outside of the organization had filed a complaint against him recently, but there hadn't been enough evidence to charge him. Hunter wouldn't be surprised if others came forward, and it was safe to say that Xavier would get some jail time.

Hunter glanced at Viviana when she sighed loudly.

She was sitting on the sofa with a cup of hot tea in her hand. He had suggested something stronger, but she insisted that the tea was fine. Especially since she claimed her workday wasn't over yet.

"What made you come back?" Viviana asked out of the blue.

"Come back from where?" he asked and strolled across the room. He sat on the table in front of her. She'd been shaken up pretty bad but seemed like herself again.

"After our meeting, you left. What made you come back?"

He lifted his cell. "I forgot my phone. I'd set it down on the chair next to where I was sitting and didn't realize I didn't have it until I got downstairs."

She nodded. "I'm glad you came back."

"Yeah, me too."

Dannette had arranged for security to shadow him just in case he got mobbed by fans when he arrived on the casino level. Only a few approached him for autographs, but then he remembered that he'd left his phone.

"Has Xavier ever come on to you like that before?" Hunter asked. He wasn't ready for the answer, but felt he needed to ask the question anyway.

She shook her head. "A few months ago, out of nowhere, he asked me out. I shut that down quick, telling him I wasn't interested. Or at least I thought I shut him down." She huffed out a breath and set the mug down. "He never put his hands on me before, though."

Hunter frowned. "He asked you out and knew you were married? I don't understand. I heard that he and Thomas were good friends. What did Thomas do when he found out that his *friend* asked you out?"

Viviana nibbled on her lower lip and looked everywhere but at him.

"Vivi?"

She rubbed her forehead, then stood abruptly and moved away from him. "I–I really don't want to talk about this, Hunter. Not right now."

He remembered her alluding to the fact that her marriage wasn't what it seemed, and now he was really curious. Maybe it was time they had the talk that they should've had seven years ago.

An idea formed in his mind, and he moved to where she was standing behind her desk. It was as if she was using it as a shield to keep him at bay. It wasn't going to work. He walked around the desk and reached for her hand and pulled her close. He was glad she didn't pull away.

"Listen, I know things between us are...weird at best." He laughed and that got a smile out of her. "But if nothing else, I want us to rebuild our friendship." They'd been friends for years before they started dating and then eventually got engaged.

"I'd like that very much," she said quietly, and tears filled her eyes.

He was afraid she'd start crying again—something he wasn't good at dealing with. He hated to see the sadness in her pretty eyes.

"My mom is cooking up a feast this weekend for a mini-family reunion."

He brushed the back of his fingers along her jawline, then cupped her cheek, loving the way she leaned into his touch. Just like she used to do.

God, she was so beautiful, and the temptation to lower his mouth to hers and taste her sweet lips was almost too strong to deny. But he couldn't. Mainly because of what she had just experienced. Besides, they still had some baggage to deal with.

Until they cleared the air, they couldn't move forward personally.

"I want you and Dannette to come by Saturday and spend the day with us," he said. "It'll only be my immediate family and a handful of friends."

When she started shaking her head, he continued. "Don't say no, Vivi. My mom would love to see you, and I'd like for you and me to get reacquainted. Besides, some of my teammates will be there, and I'd bet money that Dannette would want to meet them. She's single, right?"

A slow smile spread across Viviana's lush lips, and that urge to kiss her grew even stronger, if that was possible. Hunter swallowed hard, forcing himself to not act on the desire racing through him.

"Yeah, she's single, and she would kill me if she found out that you invited her to meet some of your teammates, and I said no."

"So don't say no. I promise you two will have a good time.

Plus, your presence would make my mom happy." That part was true. His mother adored Viviana.

She nodded. "It would be great to see her again. Okay, we'll come."

"Good. I'm looking forward to spending some time with you."

Chapter Eleven

Viviana couldn't remember the last time she had so much fun.

She and Dannette had arrived at Hunter's place early that morning, and until a few minutes ago, the action had been nonstop. Hunter wanted to get in some outdoor activities before it had gotten too hot; the day started with flag football.

After that, the women and girls broke off from the guys and jumped rope—something Viviana hadn't done since she was a kid. In between the fun and games was eating, drinking, swimming, and tons of laughter.

Now, it was early evening and she had showered and changed into a sundress that she'd brought with her. The only people left were a handful of Hunter's family and closest friends. It was a new experience for Viviana to be sitting outside on the huge deck talking with women she hadn't met until today. She never had a lot of female friends, but she could totally see being friends with these three women.

The group included Hunter's sister-in-law, Natasha, and her sister, Alandra, who Viviana learned was a former CIA agent. Alandra was married to Quinn Hamilton, one of Malik's best friends from the Navy. The man looked intimidating as hell, with long dreadlocks and a watchful expression. But he definitely had a soft side when it came to his wife and son—Quinn Jr. It was clear how much he adored them.

Also, there was another friend of theirs—Olivia Miller—a world-renowned artist who was married to Malik's friend and former SEAL teammate, Cameron "Wiz" Miller. They had a set of five-year-old twins, a boy and girl. The boy was the splitting image of his dad, green eyes and all, and was all boy when it came to roughness. While their daughter was a girly-girl, who was very conscious of not getting dirty.

Dannette was across the yard under a gazebo, chatting it up with one of Hunter's teammates who had flown in earlier that day. They seemed to be really enjoying each other's company, and Viviana hoped it could turn into a love connection.

Laughter broke out in the small group, and she realized she had missed part of the conversation. Considering she hadn't done much socializing in the last seven years, at least not with people she liked, she was surprisingly comfortable.

Probably because Hunter wasn't nearby wreaking havoc on her senses. He, his mother, and a couple of the house staff were seeing to dinner.

Viviana smiled to herself as she thought about the last few days with him. She would be eternally grateful for him showing up when he did when she was dealing with Xavier. She didn't even want to think what could've happened in that stairwell, but Hunter had been great, both then and after the incident. The days that followed had been a blur with work and teaching him as much as she could about the business.

Never in a million years would she have thought that they could ever be cordial to each other. He'd made it a point to hang out around the office, soaking up as much knowledge about the hotel and casino as possible. Viviana was impressed with how seriously he was taking his new role as co-owner of the company, and she appreciated it.

Once the basketball season started back up, he wouldn't be in Vegas much, but she was looking forward to their partnership growing stronger.

Being around Hunter again reminded her of why she had fallen in love with him in the first place. Hunter might've been arrogant, but he had a sweet and thoughtful side that not everyone got to see. He was funny, kind, and extremely protective.

Even before they'd started dating, he always made her feel important. Like she mattered to him. Once they were a couple, all of those qualities that she'd fallen in love with multiplied. He meant everything to her, and it had almost killed her to have to walk away from him.

Viviana shook that last thought free. *Don't go there*, she told herself. She was having too much fun to let the past creep in and ruin everything. Instead, she tuned back into the conversation, and Natasha was sharing a story about her four-year-old daughter.

"I knew changes had to be made when I heard her cursing when her motorized car stopped. She said, '*dammit, I put gas in this thing. What the hell is wrong with it?*'"

All the women burst out laughing, including Viviana. She remembered that Malik had a cursing problem that he blamed on his years in the Navy.

"What did you do? What did you say?" Viviana asked. "Does your son curse, too?"

"He's only three, and so far, I haven't heard any curse words from him. As for my daughter, I told her if I ever hear her using bad words again, I was going to wash her mouth out with soap."

Alandra laughed. "Oh, my God. You sound just like Momma used to sound."

"I know, right?" Natasha grinned. "When I was done fussing at babygirl, I went off on Malik. I told him if his ass didn't clean up his language, I was leaving him, and I wasn't playing."

Olivia snorted. "Don't listen to her," she said to Viviana. "She wasn't going anywhere. They're one of those couples who can't live without each other."

"Ha! Look who's talking," Natasha fired back. "Viviana, ask her how many times she married Wiz."

Viviana's eyebrows shot up, curious about this bit of news.

Olivia's sheepish expression spoke volumes, and she said, "We're not talking about me. We're talking about Tasha. But since you're putting my business out there..." she laughed and glanced at Viviana. "I married him twice."

"So that you get a better understanding of the story," Alandra added, "the two of them grew up together and were best friends from day one. They married after high school, reluctantly divorced—I'll let her or Wiz tell you about that—and then married again. But let me just say, when I first met Olivia, they were divorced, but you wouldn't have known it. They were together all the time...like a married couple! It was strange."

Olivia laughed and nudged Alandra's arm. "Stop! I know you're not calling us strange. You and Quinn win the prize for strange relationships."

"Okay, that's true," Alandra said on a laugh. "It would take forever for all of us to tell you what each one of us went through with our husbands. But one thing is for sure, once you're theirs, you're theirs, and there is no walking away from them."

"Despite the challenges of us getting our happily-ever-afters, our men love hard and fiercely," Natasha said, staring lovingly out at the huge pool where their husbands and the kids were hanging out.

"And we wouldn't have it any other way," Olivia added.

Natasha leaned in and whispered, "So, with that said, what's up with you and my brother-in-law? If you're here, I'm assuming you guys have made peace?"

If her skin wasn't so dark, Viviana was sure her cheeks would be cherry red. She had no idea what they knew about her situation with Hunter, and she wasn't sure what to say.

Peals of laughter floated from the pool area, immediately breaking the awkward silence. Viviana released a sigh of relief when everyone's attention turned to the pool area.

"Mommy, look!" Quinn Jr. said to Alandra. He couldn't have been more than four or five and was standing on the edge of the pool, looking as if he was getting ready to dive in.

"Okay, baby, let me see what you can do," Alandra encouraged as she sipped her cocktail.

Viviana didn't know how she could be so calm. She'd be a nervous wreck if she had kids and they were diving into a pool. His father was in the pool nearby. Still, not close enough for her comfort.

From what Viviana had been told, all of the kids had learned to swim before they were walking—no doubt because all of their fathers were former SEALS.

"All right, everyone. Dinner is served," Hunter's mother said as she, Hunter, and a couple of house staff strolled out with more food. They had been coming out periodically and setting dishes on two long tables against the back wall of the deck.

Viviana's gaze immediately went to Hunter, who was carrying a huge pan of barbecue. She watched as his muscles contracted with each move he made. The light-blue T-shirt he was wearing didn't hide much. It showed off his muscular biceps and emphasized his broad shoulders and wide chest.

The man had always been fit, with practically zero body fat, but it seemed he was more muscular than she remembered.

As if sensing her watching him, Hunter glanced at her. Viviana's heart flipped and practically leaped out of her chest when he winked and smiled at her.

Good Lord. No wonder all of the groupies fell at his feet. The man could make a woman weak in the knees by just flashing his pearly whites. He had her all twisted up inside and all he'd done was wink and smile.

How was it possible that she was falling for him all over again? Then again, if she was honest with herself, she had never stopped loving him. Their love affair might've been cut short, but that didn't stop her from thinking about him every day since she'd had to walk away.

Viviana swallowed hard as he headed toward her. They might've been apart for years, but she had never stopped loving him.

Was it insane to think that they could just pick up where'd they'd left off?

Yes, that little voice inside her head screamed. But her heart wasn't listening. Deep in her heart she believed that anything was possible...even rekindling a relationship with the only man she'd ever loved.

She wanted that more than she wanted her next breath. Hell, if she was given the chance to cash in her newfound wealth for a chance to be with Hunter again, she'd take it in a heartbeat. And that thought scared her a little. She didn't want to get hurt, and he was the only person in the world who had the power to crush her.

"Come on." He extended his hand to her, and she grabbed on, letting him pull her from her seat. "Let's fix a plate before my brother and the others dig in. Otherwise, we'll be left with scraps."

Viviana laughed. She wasn't that hungry, but the closer she got to the huge spread of food, she figured she could eat a little something...or a lot.

Hunter slowed before they reached the others who were already at the food, and Viviana glanced up at him.

"What?" she said when all he did was stare down at her.

"I just want you to know that I'm glad you're here," he said sincerely, still holding her hand. "I'm also glad you're back in my life...in any capacity. I've missed you."

Viviana's pulse amped up, and her chest tightened. He had no idea how much it meant to hear him say that. She had missed him like crazy, and there'd been many times when she didn't think she could go on without him in her life. Granted, he wasn't making any promises, but right now, she'd take whatever he was offering.

"Yeah, me too," she said, and decided that as soon as he was ready to hear her story, she'd tell him why she'd had to leave him all those years ago.

I just hope I don't lose him again.

Chapter Twelve

As Hunter poured himself another drink, he watched Viviana from across the room. She was standing on the balcony off of the game room, staring out at the mountains in the distance.

After dinner, a few of them, including her, headed to the game room, but Hunter wanted her to himself. He finally was ready to hear her tell him why she'd left him for Thomas.

He just wasn't sure she was ready to talk.

He carried the drinks to the balcony. "Here you go," he said, handing her the water. "Are you sure you don't want something a little stronger?"

"Nah, I already had two glasses of wine, but thank you." She gave him a timid smile and turned back to the mountains.

He leaned against the railing and sipped his drink, watching the sun slowly slip behind the mountains. "You look deep in thought. What's on your mind?" he asked.

"I was just thinking about how peaceful it is out here. I can barely see the neighbors' houses. Have you rented this place before?"

"No, but I heard that it's for sale. You interested?"

She cracked a smile. "I do need to move out of Dannette's place, but this is way too big for one person. I'm thinking about taking one of the suites at the hotel and living in it."

"Hmm, that's an interesting idea. Are you sure you want to live that close to work? You're already a workaholic. Living that close, you might never leave the office."

She turned to him, those beautiful eyes sparkling under the dim evening sky.

He wanted her.

Damn. He wanted to carry her into the house, away from prying eyes, and love on her incredible body.

He wanted to remind her of how good things used to be between them.

But he couldn't. At least not until he knew the truth about her and Thomas.

"You always did know me better than anyone," she said softly. "And you're right, me living in the hotel is a horrible idea."

They both laughed. He loved when she laughed, and based on the little he'd garnered from Dannette, Viviana hadn't been happy in a long time. He wanted to know why.

"There's so much I don't know about you, and I think it's time we changed that," Hunter said. "We need to talk."

She stared at him for so long without responding that he thought she wouldn't, but then she said, "Okay."

Okay. The word was spoken so quietly he barely heard her.

"Listen." He slid his free arm around her and let his hand rest on the small of her back as he leaned in close. "If you're not ready to tell—"

"I've wanted to tell you from the day I had to leave. You're right, Hunter, it's time." She glanced down at the water bottle that she was gripping tightly with two hands. "I need you to know that I never wanted to—"

"Not here," he interrupted and reached for her hand. "Come with me and we'll go somewhere a little more private."

They walked back into the room just as Dannette was coming to them.

"Hey, I'm gonna go to a club with Scott, but I don't want you to have to drive home alone," her friend said. "Are you almost ready to go? I can have him pick me up from my place."

Viviana squeezed Hunter's hand and he glanced at her, but she was still looking at Dannette.

"I'm going to stick around a little longer, and I'll be fine going back to your place alone. Go, have fun, and I'll see you later."

Dannette's eyebrows dipped into a frown, and her gaze bounced from him back to Viviana again. "You sure? I don't have to—"

"I'll make sure she gets home safely," Hunter said.

"And if I'm going to be really late, I'll call you," Viviana added. "Now go and quit worrying about me. I'm fine."

They said their goodbyes, and Hunter guided Viviana to his wing of the house. He wasn't sure what all she was going to tell him, but he didn't want any interruptions.

"Do you want something else to eat? We can go downstairs and grab something," he said, stopping at the circular staircase.

"Are you kidding? I ate enough to last a week. I don't think I could eat anything else, even if I wanted to." She patted her flat stomach.

She was thinner than he remembered, but she still had a slammin' body.

They walked down the hallway, past the guest rooms until they came to another short hallway.

"Man, this place is bigger than I originally thought," Viviana said.

"Yeah, it's amazing. Wait until you see the master suite." He felt her stiffen, then slow down, and he quickly added, "Don't worry. We're going to hang out in the attached sitting room."

A few seconds later, they were at the door. Instead of going right in, Hunter stopped them just outside of it.

"I was only thinking about us having some privacy, which was why I thought of the space I was using. But if you'll be more comfortable talking somewhere else in the house, that can be arranged."

"No...this is fine."

He still felt her unease. "Sweetheart, nothing's going to happen. We're just talking."

"I know, I'm just..." She sighed loudly. "To be honest, I'm nervous. I've always wanted to have this conversation with you, but it's not an easy one, Hunter."

"I know, and I won't rush you. I'll let you tell me what you want me to know, and we'll go from there. Okay?"

She nodded and they entered his space. He closed and locked the door behind them. His room was away from everyone else's, and before anyone came looking for him, they'd probably text him first.

"Wow, this is like a small apartment," Viviana said, looking around in awe.

"Yeah, it's tricked out nice. It's a large one-bedroom suite. Feel free to look around."

Hunter watched as she strolled past the tiny kitchen and dining area that overlooked the sitting room.

"To your right is the bedroom, and you can get to the bathroom from inside the room and from out here," he said, pushing open a door that led to the spa-like bathroom.

"I've seen some large homes, and even lived in one, but this might be the biggest I've seen to date. I love everything about it," Viviana said, glancing into the bedroom before moving back into the sitting area.

"Is that water enough for you?" Hunter asked. "I have a bottle of bourbon in one of the cabinets, and a couple of beers in the refrigerator."

"I'm good right now," she said, taking a seat on the sofa.

Instead of sitting beside her, he sat in the chair next to her.

"I'm not sure where to start," she said nervously.

"How about at the beginning?" Hunter suggested. He rarely got nervous, but he braced himself for whatever she planned to tell him.

"I never loved him. I hated Thomas more than I thought I could ever hate anyone," she said quietly, but with so much conviction that Hunter felt it to his bones. Her voice trembled with each word and he could see how hard this was for her. "He blackmailed me, and at the time, I felt I didn't have a choice. I had to marry him."

Shock and anger collided inside of Hunter, and he tried to keep his emotions in check. He had already thought Thomas was the lowest form of human life, but now, seeing the anguish on Viviana's face, Hunter questioned whether the man was even human.

He started to reach for Viviana, but stopped himself. Though he wanted to pull her into his arms and hold her tightly, he didn't want to say or do anything that would stop her from talking. He needed to know why she'd betrayed him...why she gave up everything to marry that asshole.

"What did he blackmail you with?" he asked.

"My mother."

Hunter jolted, and dread seeped into his body at the mention of her mother. The woman was toxic. Yet, she had always had some type of mental or emotional control over Viviana. She was a master manipulator, and though Viviana was one of the sharpest women Hunter knew, she was no match for Chandra Connelly.

"She owed a loan shark a lot of money that she couldn't pay back. They gave her three days to come up with the money. Otherwise, they threatened to kill her."

Hunter almost felt guilty that his first thought was that she should've let her die. Because that's what Chandra would've done, had it been Viviana in that situation. She might've been her mother, but there was no way she could've loved Viviana with all of the shit she put her through over the years.

"So, what I'm hearing is that you left me because of money?" He tried to keep the bitterness out of his tone, but failed. "That doesn't make sense. You know I would've given you anything you wanted or needed. *Anything*. Baby, all you had to do was ask, and it would've been yours. But you knew that. Help me understand why you went to Thomas."

"I didn't. My mother did." She finally looked at him and seeing the anguish in her eyes was like taking a punch to the gut. "She owed four hundred thousand dollars. I have no idea why anyone would let her debt get that high, but—"

"If the loan shark knew she had a connection to me—you," Hunter said pointedly, "they would've assumed that I'd pay. And for you, I would've."

Viviana set the water bottle down and leaned forward with her elbows on her thighs. She wrung her hands together as seconds ticked by before she spoke again.

"You told me the last time that you bailed my mother out of a jam would be the last time. You said that you would *never* give her another penny and that she could rot in hell for all you cared."

Damn. He had said that and a whole lot more. But there

was no way he could've said no to Viviana, and she knew that. Yet, she chose to let Thomas blackmail her.

"I didn't want whatever crap my mother was involved in to affect your career again," she said as if reading his mind. "You remember what happened the last time, right?"

Hunter didn't respond. Of course, he remembered.

He could've gotten kicked out of the league. After he'd given Chandra money to pay off her debts, she came back for more. When he vowed to never give her another dime, she went to the media with lies.

Yeah, he would never forget that time in his life. She had told anyone who would listen that he placed bets on NBA games.

The league hated the negative attention that they were getting because of him. They didn't tolerate shit like that and he thought for sure his career was over, especially when they told him to take some time off and get his personal life in order.

He had gone through hell trying to prove that his future mother-in-law was lying. It wasn't until Viviana begged her mother to retract her claims did the situation get straightened out.

"I couldn't let you go through anything else like that because of my mother," Viviana said in a small voice. "She went to Thomas, begging him to help her out because she couldn't come to us. He used that opportunity to blackmail me and to hurt you."

Hunter lunged out of his seat and almost threw his drink across the room, but stopped himself. Instead, he slammed back the rest of the dark liquid and went to the kitchen for another. The short walk gave him a moment to tamp down his anger.

"He's always been jealous of you," she continued. "And when we got engaged, he said that he was determined to take me away from you."

Instead of returning to his seat, he placed his hands, palms down on the kitchen counter and asked, "What was the agreement between you and my brother? Besides marrying him, what else did you have to do to fulfill your part of the deal?" he choked out, afraid of how much of her soul she had to sacrifice for that monster.

When she didn't respond, Hunter glanced at her and saw that she was wiping tears from her face. If his stepbrother hadn't already been dead, Hunter would...

He let the thought trail off because thinking like that wasn't doing him or anyone else any good. There was nothing he could do to Thomas except stomp on his grave.

He was dead, and Hunter hoped he rotted in hell.

"Besides leaving you the note, I had to cut all ties, give up my cell phone, and promise to never contact you again. Then I had to agree to marry him and stay married for ten years. That would clear my mother's debt and..."

She stopped abruptly and placed her hand on the front of her neck as if struggling to breathe. But then her sobs reached his ears. Deep sobs that rattled her whole body and cut straight to his heart.

He never could handle her tears, but this was different. She was hurting, and he felt her pain. He hated that he was forcing her to relive the hell that Thomas had inflicted on her. But they had to get it all out in the open if they were ever going to move past this nightmare.

"Vivi...sweetheart... What other debt were you paying off?" He inched closer as she wiped feverishly at the tears streaming down her cheeks. "Tell me the rest."

"He said that if I tried to leave him before the ten years was up, he would kill you."

Hunter stood with his mouth gaping open. "He told you

that?" There had never been any love between him and Thomas, but he had no idea the guy hated him that much.

"Yes. He had photos...with timestamps. Days leading up to him blackmailing me, he'd been having you followed, even when you were on the road."

Hunter shook his head. *Damn him.*

"He said that in ten years, you would move on, forget about me, and marry someone else. He thought that would also be enough time for me to fall in love with him," she spat.

Her distress was replaced with anger and like with moments ago when he felt her every emotion, this was no difference. Her fury was palpable.

"Every day I was with him, I hated him more and more. When we were in public, I had to pretend we had a good marriage. I never wanted to be with him!" she cried. "*Never!* I only wanted you. I only wanted you," she repeated over and over hysterically until her words came out in a rasp.

"Aww, baby..." Hunter hurried to her and wrapped her in his arms just as Viviana's legs gave out. He lifted her, and she clung to him.

Carrying her to the sofa, Hunter's heart broke as she trembled against him. She wouldn't stop crying. He could feel hot tears splashing against his skin with her face buried in the crook of his neck.

"Come on, Vivi. You gotta stop crying. You know I can't handle your tears." He hated seeing her like this.

When he neared the sofa, she tightened her arms around his neck and her legs were around his waist. She probably thought he would release her, but he had no intention of doing that. He didn't want to let her go, and he sat on the sofa with her cradled to his body.

"Look at me," he said, and cupped her face between his hands, forcing her to look at him. "I'm so sorry for what you went through." He placed a kiss on her forehead, her cheeks, and then her lips. "I am so, so sorry, baby."

Hunter knew there was probably more she hadn't told him, but right now, he just wanted to hold her, to comfort her, and to promise her that things would get better.

He rocked with her, trying to ignore the way their bodies were hugged up together and how amazing she felt. It was hard, though.

When he picked her up and carried her to the sofa, it had been with good intentions, but now... His body was responding to her nearness. Her dress was hiked up and his dick pushed uncomfortably against his zipper right at the apex of her thighs. She felt so damn good, and it was like a sweet torture. He might have to get some distance between them so that he could think straight.

"I never stopped loving you, Hunter," she mumbled, speaking the words that he was feeling. "I never stopped loving you." Her teary-eyed gaze cut him deep, and he ached at seeing the sadness in her red eyes. "I never stopped loving you," she said again and again.

"I know, baby. Me too." Still cupping her face, he wiped her tears with the pads of his thumbs. He touched his mouth to hers, giving her a quick peck on the lips before he said, "You were always mine, and you always will be."

He meant every word. He thought he would die when she'd left him, but now she was back. He was never letting her go again. She was his. Always was, always would be.

This time when Hunter kissed her, he covered her mouth with his, hoping she could feel everything that he felt in his heart. She was a part of him, had always been a part of him. Which was why he had never been able to get serious with another woman. No one ever felt right because she was the only one for him.

God, he had missed her...missed this. Holding her, tasting her, he would never get enough of having her in his arms again.

Viviana fisted the front of his shirt, pulling him even closer, as their mouths frantically mated. They were breathing hard, and then their hands clawed at each other's clothes, struggling to get out of them.

Hunter didn't know where they went from here, mentally, or emotionally, but physically, he wanted her. And by the way she was attacking him with her mouth and hands, she wanted him, too.

How the hell would they ever pick up the pieces of their lives after losing so many years? He had no clue. What he did know, though, was that they were going to be together forever.

I'm never letting her go again...

Chapter Thirteen

Viviana's breath came in short spurts as their kiss grew frantic, and she craved more of Hunter. It was as if her body had a mind of its own. She couldn't stop herself from rotating her hips and grinding against his erection. It was lined up perfectly with her opening, and he felt so good and hard.

The barriers stopping her from sliding onto his shaft were her panties and the khaki shorts that he was still wearing. But the material caused just enough tantalizing friction against her to make the sexual throbbing between her thighs even more intense.

Before jerking his mouth from hers, Hunter squeezed her butt and growled against her lips. "I want you so bad," he said, gasping for air. "But if this is too soon or you want to wait, tell me now."

Viviana wanted him more than a starving woman wanted her next meal. It had been so long...too long since she'd been with a man, and when that man was Hunter, there was no way she didn't want this. Everything in her was about to combust and he had barely touched her.

"I want this, and I want what we had," she said emphatically. Her voice was almost pleading. She knew it was probably too soon to have sex with him, but her body longed for his touch. She needed him. No way were they stopping. "I want *you*," she insisted.

"That's all I needed to hear."

She gasped when Hunter suddenly stood with her in his arms, as if she weighed nothing. While carrying her to his bedroom, he continued to kiss her, caressing her lips with his and stirring her passion that was threatening to break free.

The more he made love to her mouth, the more anxious she became. It wasn't that she was nervous, but knowing that after so many years apart, they would finally be together intimately again, was overwhelming.

Once they were near the bed, Hunter pulled his mouth from hers and reached down to yank back the covers. Viviana didn't want to let him go when he began to lay her on the bed, but she relented as anticipation ratcheted up inside of her.

Hunter wasted no time in stepping out of his khaki shorts, but before tossing them to the floor, he dug his wallet out of the back pocket. She watched his every move, unable to stop looking at him, even when he pulled out a foil packet and tossed it onto the nightstand.

Viviana's heartbeat kicked into overdrive when he dropped the shorts to the floor. The man's body was a work of art. Broad shoulders, muscular pecs and arms, he was chiseled to perfection, and the gray boxer briefs he was wearing highlighted one of his best assets.

She could see why he had an endorsement deal with the underwear company. The briefs hugged his lower body and accentuated his big dick that was barely contained behind the material.

Viviana sucked in a breath when he slid the briefs down his long, muscular legs, and his erection was on full display, springing to attention. Thick and long, *my goodness*, he was truly a sight. Her hammering heart felt as if it was going to burst from her chest.

She could barely remember the last time she'd been in his bed, and tonight she wanted them to take their time. But her body was humming with long-awaited need.

When she glanced up, Hunter was watching her, and his gaze swept down her half-naked body.

"God, you are so beautiful," he murmured in awe, and was looking at her as if he'd never seen her before.

She was thinner than she'd been when they were together, but other than that, not much had changed.

"But I want to see the rest of you," he said as he slipped his fingers into the waistband of her panties. Viviana lifted her hips, allowing him to tug the lacy garment down her legs. "Man, you're breathtaking."

A wave of excitement swirled inside of her, knowing that they were about to do what she'd dreamed about even years after they'd parted ways.

Hunter dropped her undies on the floor and climbed onto the bed next to her.

"I want you so bad, but I don't want to rush this," he said roughly before capturing her mouth with his.

Their tongues mated as his large hand glided down the side of her body, caressing and squeezing along the way. He moved more on top of her, and Viviana ran her palms over his head, loving how soft his hair felt under her touch.

Pulse pounding loudly in her ears, she kissed him with everything in her. And Viviana was sure she wouldn't be able to hang on long, but she wanted to. God, she wanted to. She wanted to savor this moment with him and enjoy every second of the joining of their bodies.

Hunter eased his mouth from hers. "Mmm, you smell so good," he murmured against her skin and slowly kissed his way to the area behind her ear.

Goodness. He still remembered how to get her worked up.

She shouldn't be surprised. Back in the day, he knew her body better than she knew her own. And he knew that the spot behind her ear was one of her most sensitive areas. He lingered there for a minute, kissing and licking before moving down her neck. Tingles of pleasure shot straight to the soles of her feet.

Viviana wasn't sure how much more she could take. The way he was kissing her, touching her, and making her feel a desire that she hadn't felt in years, was almost her undoing.

Seven years. It had been over seven years since she'd been with him, and it seemed he was going to torture her with his tongue and lips before he joined their bodies.

"I've missed you, and I've missed these," he said, cupping her breasts.

"Oh," Viviana breathed, and her eyes drifted closed as he tweaked, teased, and pinched her nipples with his finger and thumb. The intense torment had her bucking against him, trying to hang on to what little control she had. "Hunter, I—I don't know how much... *Ohhh,*" she whimpered, squirming beneath him when his mouth replaced his fingers. His tongue snaked around her nipple, licking, then sucking her breast into his mouth.

"Oh, my God..." she moaned. His mouth was on one breast, while his hand squeezed and fondled the other. "I—I..." He had her so worked up, she was struggling to form a complete sentence. "I need more."

Normally she wasn't one for telling him what she wanted or needed, but her throbbing sex ached for some attention.

"Now...please. I need you. I need you inside of me," she begged.

"I guess we need the same thing, then." Hunter worked his way up her body, kissing every inch of her along the way. When he reached her lips, his kiss was so sweet and tender that she whimpered into his mouth. She loved that he was taking his time, but she couldn't handle it.

As if reading her mind, he eased his mouth from hers and snatched the condom from the nightstand. When he sat back on his haunches, her gaze immediately went to his thick length, and excitement pumped through her veins.

Her heart rate amped up in anticipation of what was to follow.

She was with Hunter, the only man she had ever loved, and they were really going to do this.

While he sheathed himself, a burning desire gleamed in his dark eyes and sent heat charging through her body. Viviana squirmed under his watchful gaze, and the passion swirling inside of her grew more intense.

He hadn't even entered her and already she was panting for air.

"Relax, baby," he said, and leaned down, teasing her mouth with his sweet kisses. "Just relax."

Apparently, he knew she was wound tightly, but she couldn't help...

"Hunter." She gasped into his mouth, and her back bowed off the bed when he slid a finger inside of her, and then another. "Oh, my..."

Her nails dug into his muscular biceps and her thighs squeezed closed around his hand, locking his arm in place. But that didn't stop his fingers from sliding in and out of her and picking up speed with each thrust. And just when she started to reach the edge of her control, he removed his hand and settled his large body between her thighs.

The head of his dick bumped against her opening, and Viviana stiffened involuntarily.

Hunter froze.

"Vivi—"

"Don't stop, please don't stop." She didn't care if she was begging. She needed and wanted him more than he knew. Her vibrator had served her well over the years, but no machine or any other man would ever satisfy her the way she knew Hunter could.

Concern radiated from his eyes.

"Please," she said, and cupped his face to pull him close to her mouth. "Don't stop."

While kissing him, she started rotating her hips, and brushing up against his length. A low groan rumbled inside of him, and he grabbed hold of her left thigh, lifted it slightly, and slowly eased between her slick folds.

Inch by delicious inch, he filled her completely.

"Yes," Viviana breathed as her body adjusted around his thick shaft.

Everything about Hunter was huge, and she marveled at how perfectly they fit together. They continued kissing as he started driving in and out of her, going deeper with each thrust. Viviana picked up the rhythm and matched his moves, stroke for stroke.

He felt so damn good, stirring the passion that raged through her body as his thrusts grew more demanding. Viviana widened her thighs, wanting to feel even more of him, and Hunter ripped his mouth from hers with a growl.

She was barely hanging on as he pounded into her like a man possessed.

"Yes, yes, yes," she chanted, her head thrashing against the pillow as she fisted the sheet on each side of her. A wave of ecstasy whirled around inside of her, and she struggled to hang on. "Hu—Hunter," she whimpered.

"I'm right here, baby. I'm right here," he ground out, pumping into her with more speed and power.

Her body tightened, and all rational thought flew from her mind after one last forceful thrust had her bucking against him. Her orgasm came hard and fast, jostling and twisting her up inside before propelling her over the proverbial cliff.

Hunter was right behind her, growling his release before he collapsed on top of her.

"*Damn...*" he panted, breathing hard against her ear, and as if suddenly remembering she was under him, he quickly lifted up.

"Are you...are you okay?" he asked between breaths and kissed her lips before staring down at her from beneath hooded eyes.

Too exhausted and unable to find her voice, Viviana swallowed, then nodded.

But inside she was doing a fist pump and screaming, *Hell yeah! I'm better than okay. That was great!*

Chapter Fourteen

Oh, my God... I just had sex with Hunter. I just had sex with Hunter. The words played over and over in Viviana's mind.

He was lying right next to her. Yet, it was still hard to believe it. Ever since he came back into her life, each moment felt surreal. It was like wishing for something for so long, then all of a sudden, what she'd been yearning for was right there. Viviana just hoped she wasn't dreaming, because if she was, she never wanted to wake up.

Hunter lifted onto his elbow and stared down at her. "Are you sure you're okay?" He caressed her cheek lovingly. "I didn't hurt you, did I?"

Viviana gave him a tired smile and ran a finger over his forehead to wipe away the worry lines. She was a little sore, but that was nothing compared to how satisfied he'd made her.

"No, I'm fine." Actually, she was better than fine—exhausted but exhilarated at the same time.

"You would tell me if you weren't, right?"

Still smiling, she nodded.

"Okay, then give me a minute, and I'll be right back."

As he climbed out of bed and headed to the bathroom to dispose of the condom, Viviana admired his firm backside and super-long legs. *Whew! What a body.* His intense workout regimen and running up and down the basketball court for a living had definitely helped sculpt every inch of his tall frame.

Sighing in contentment, her eyes were starting to drift close when the bathroom door opened, and Hunter walked out, still naked as the day he was born. Her gaze traveled over his broad chest, flat abs, and then lower. He'd never been shy about his body. Why should he be? The man was built like a stallion and hung like one, too.

When he climbed back into bed, he adjusted the pillow beneath his head, then pulled her into his arms. This was exactly where Viviana wanted to be, and she snuggled against him with her head on his chest and her arm across his stomach. She never imagined that they'd be in bed together again. Hell, she never thought they'd ever be on speaking terms. Yet, here they were, and this was the happiest she'd been in a long time.

Hunter ran his hand gently up and down her hip, lulling her into a state of peace. She really was tired–emotionally and physically. The last few days had been draining, with both good and bad moments. But those instances brought her and Hunter back together, and she wouldn't change anything.

Hunter cleared his throat. "I'm not sure how to ask this, but when was the last time you—"

"I never had sex with Thomas, if that's what you're wondering." Viviana knew he was asking because she was tight when he tried to enter her, and it had given him pause. She glanced up at him to find him staring down at her. "I couldn't. I didn't love him. I didn't even like him. There was no way I could've slept with him."

"You never slept with him?" he asked, shock dripping from each word.

She shook her head. "We went to Lake Tahoe after a quickie wedding at his house in Vegas. We stayed in a suite. He slept in the bed and I slept on the sofa. It was the same when I lived with him. There was a sitting room off of his bedroom. For the most part, that was my room. The only time I didn't sleep in there was when—which was rare—the staff had off. Then I slept in the guest room."

Hunter gave his head a shake as if trying to understand. "Wow...I'm shocked. Did he ever try to...try to force himself on you?" he asked hesitantly, as if bracing himself for the answer.

"No. He was a lot of things, but he never tried to force me to have sex or take advantage of me. I found out in the letter he left me that, after a year of marriage and no sex, he started sleeping around. He and a woman had a child six months ago. That's who he left the house and staff to."

Hunter sat up fast, catching her off guard and forcing her to fall back on the bed. She laughed and looked at him.

"The more you tell me about the guy, the more I feel like I never knew him. You didn't know about the kid?"

"Nope, and I don't care. If I was sleeping with him, it would be a different story, but that wasn't the case. I feel bad for the child. As for the house–I hated it about as much as I disliked him."

Hunter shook his head and laid back down, pulling her against him.

Wanting to finish telling him about the marriage contract, she continued.

"The two things that I wasn't budging on regarding the contract was sex and keeping my name. There was no way I'd accept Thomas's name. I was afraid he would insist and then I'd have to decide what to do about you and my mother, but he went along with it. Some people referred to me as Mrs. Reagan, but on paper, I'm still Viviana Connelly."

From the day she and Hunter started dating, she never considered having anyone's last name but his. She had been looking forward to getting married and becoming Viviana Graham. She used to imagine being called Mrs. Graham.

A full minute passed before Hunter said, "I don't know what to say. I know you didn't love him—"

"I hated him," she said with force. "Sometimes I would let him hold my hand or allow him to hug me on occasion when we were in public to keep up appearances, but that's it."

Hunter gave his head a little shake. "I can't believe you two never had sex in seven years."

"At first, Thomas tried, thinking he would change my mind, but I'd remind him of the contract. He'd say something like, *eventually you're going to be begging for a man's touch, and I'll be right here.* I never wanted him or anyone who wasn't you, and he eventually got the message."

Hunter didn't say anything. She might've remained celibate while they were a part, but she had no doubt that he'd been with other women.

As an NBA superstar, his female fans used to throw themselves at him, even though they knew he was engaged. She definitely didn't want to know who all he'd been with since. Besides, she had no right. She had left him.

"You were my first...and my last," Viviana said.

Hunter rolled on top of her and gazed into her eyes. "From now on, it's just you and me, baby. I didn't plan tonight, but I'm not sorry. I hope you—"

"I'm not sorry, either," Viviana hurried to say. She cupped his cheek and ran the pad of her thumb over the light stubble on his jaw. "I wanted you, Hunter, and I've missed you so much."

He lowered his head and kissed her slowly. The kiss was so sweet and tender it made her whimper. God, she had missed this man. Seemed like they both had been saying that a lot today.

"I know we can't pick up where we left off," Hunter said against her mouth before he lifted his head, "but I want us to try."

"I want that, too." It was scary and exciting that they were going to give themselves another try. Before she'd had to break things off with him, their relationship had been perfect. Hunter was everything she'd ever wanted in a man. Granted, they were different people now, but she just hoped they could get back to that point.

"I'm getting ready to jump in the shower. How about joining me?" he said, a wicked grin covering his sexy lips.

Viviana smiled up at him, recalling all the showers they'd taken together in the past. Suddenly, she wasn't as tired as she'd been a moment ago.

"Sounds like fun."

A few minutes later, Hunter stood and lifted Viviana from the bed. She'd never been heavy, but he was concerned about just how much of a lightweight she had become. Considering how he loved eating, he was going to enjoy feeding her and putting a little more meat back on her bones.

"You know you don't have to carry me, right?" Viviana said, though her arm was around his neck and her head rested comfortably against his shoulder.

Hunter strolled across the room with her in his arms. "I know, but I like the feel of your naked body hugged up against mine. You wouldn't want to take that pleasure from me, would you?"

She gave him a sleepy grin. "Definitely not, and I shamelessly love it when you carry me around."

"Good to know." He entered the huge bathroom and set her on her feet next to the luxurious shower that could accommodate at least five more people easily.

"Wow, this thing is massive. I guess it fits right in, considering the size of everything else in this house. Do you know the owner of this place?"

"Not personally, but he's a retired NBA player," Hunter said, turning on one of the showerheads.

There were three heads in the supersized shower, one being a ceiling-mounted sprayer. There was also a digital water temperature controller, a travertine bench, and strategically placed massage sprayers as well as steam sauna settings.

That feature was something he intended to add to his shower at his house. Those features would be perfect to come home to after a physically draining basketball game.

Hunter adjusted the water until it reached a comfortable temperature, then pulled her inside the glass enclosure.

"Ahh, hell. I don't have a shower cap for you," he said, and started to move her away from the spray of water, but Viviana stopped him.

"It's okay. Now that I wear my hair natural, I'm not as concerned about getting it wet like I used to be."

That brought a smile to Hunter's face. They'd made love plenty of times in the shower, and he always had to be careful of getting her relaxed hair wet.

"In that case..." He moved them both to where they were directly under the showerhead and Viviana shrieked. She hurried from under the spray and bumped into him, and might've fallen if he hadn't grabbed her around the waist.

"Damn, baby. It's just water," he teased, and they both burst out laughing.

"It's cold!" She slapped him against his chest, and he grabbed her hand before she removed it from his body. He brought her palm up to his lips and placed a kiss in the center of it.

"Sorry, it should be warm enough now," he said, backing her up until they both were beneath the sprayer.

She sighed and said, "That's nice."

Hunter stared into her upturned face and his heart swelled with so much emotion as their gazes connected. "Did I mention that I'm glad you're here and that I've missed you?"

She gave him a sweet smile and eased one hand around his waist and the other down his body until she made contact with his shaft. She squeezed him, and he sucked in a breath.

"I think you did...a few times. The feeling is mutual. It almost doesn't seem real," she said. She peppered kisses over his wet chest as she slid her hand slowly up and down his length, stroking him until he grew thick in her grasp.

He hoped she was okay with a quickie, because this round definitely wasn't going to last long.

"I guess I should show you just how real the moment is."

Hunter slipped one hand behind her neck, and the other went around her waist as he covered her mouth with his. He planned to continue expressing himself with words regarding his feelings for her, but he also wanted to show her just how much he had missed her.

Their kiss started out teasingly, but quickly turned heated as their tongues tangled. He backed her against the wall and lifted her off the floor. His dick was in position to enter her, but he pulled up short.

"Shit, I almost—"

"I'm on the pill," Viviana blurted, and her arms tightened

around his neck as she rubbed her sex against him, clearly trying to scratch an itch.

She felt so damn good, and Hunter struggled to keep himself from diving into her. He never had sex without a condom...except for with her. They'd been together for years before they weren't, and like in so many ways, she was his one and only.

"I'm clean," he said and forced himself to slowly slide into her sweet heat. She was still so tight, but...*shit*, she felt incredible and snug around his dick. It was a struggle not to pound into her like a madman. He wanted to do this over and over again, but that wouldn't be possible if he hurt her.

"You're not going to hurt me," Viviana said as if reading his mind. "I want you. *All* of you, and I want it hard and fast."

Well, hell. That's all he needed to hear...

"Hold on," he said gruffly, and gripped the back of her thighs, lifting her up a little higher. Her mouth formed a perfect "O" when he started sliding her up and down his length.

He was glad she wanted it hard and fast, because the erotic sounds that she was making with each thrust was making him crazy. He went deeper, burying himself inside of her as far as he could go, and loving how her muscles contracted around him.

His fingers dug into her thighs as he lifted her up and down his length, going deeper and faster. Her full breasts bounced with each move and rubbed against his chest, sending a blast of heat rocketing through him. There was no way in hell he could last much longer, but he definitely didn't want to come before she did.

As if on cue, Viviana cried out his name while her body shuddered against him, and her nails dug into his shoulders. Hunter loved watching her fall apart in his arms, with her head back and her eyes tightly closed. It made his impending orgasm build, growing more powerful by the second as he pounded in and out of her harder and even faster.

"Hunter!" Viviana screamed when hit with another orgasm, and Hunter lost it.

His release slammed into him so strong and powerful, that it almost brought him to his knees. Breathing hard and chest heaving, he tightened his hold on her and pressed her back against the tiled wall for extra support.

"Damn, that was intense," he mumbled against her neck, still struggling to catch his breath. Seemed she was having the same problem if the way her pulse was pounding was any indication.

She dropped her forehead to his shoulder, and her body went limp in his arms. "Yep, that was intense. You wore me out."

Hunter chuckled. "I could say the same about you. How about we get cleaned up, take a little nap, and go for round three?"

Viviana sputtered a laugh. "Good, Lord. You're insatiable... but okay. I'm game."

Chapter Fifteen

The next morning, Hunter woke before Viviana, and he stared down at her sleeping form. A smile touched his lips as he thought about how he'd feasted on her luscious body the night before. It was like old times. They had always been good together, and they still had that same incredible connection.

He was thankful that she was back in his life, and he planned to fight like hell to keep it that way. Viviana was the only woman for him. He'd known it before, and he knew it even more now. She'd been through emotional hell, and he had every intention of making sure the rest of her life was like a dream come true.

Seven years. She hadn't had sex in seven years.

It was no wonder she had been so tight when he first entered her. He had come close to stopping for fear of hurting her, but with her urging, he hadn't.

She never had sex with Thomas.

That was good. It hadn't been on his mind when they were in the heat of the moment, but now that he knew, it made their reunion that much more special. He believed her when she'd told him that she hadn't wanted anyone but him—but knowing she had abstained from sex meant everything.

You were my first and my last.

He loved knowing that he was her only. But at the same time, he felt like shit that he couldn't say the same.

It's not how you start, but how you finish, he remembered the swimmer, Michael Phelps, saying after winning several Olympic gold medals. Going forward—that's what Hunter planned to keep in mind as he and Viviana moved forward.

Hunter glanced toward the television that was mounted on the wall across from the bed. His photo was on the screen, and the sports commentators were talking about him, and from what he could tell, it wasn't good.

This was why he rarely watched these sports shows. Sure, it was great to hear them sing him praises, but too often they found something negative about him to discuss.

He turned up the volume enough to hear, but not enough to wake Viviana.

"I mean come on, man. If someone left me a casino, I'd accept it too," one of them said. *He was a former NFL defensive end. "What's he supposed to say, 'thanks but no thanks, I can't take it?'"*

"I'm not saying that, but the guy has a gambling problem," the other one, a former NBA player, said.

"Allegedly he has a gambling problem. Don't forget, he has maintained over the years that he just enjoys gambling. He's not addicted."

"That's right," Hunter mumbled and wanted to give the guy a fist bump.

"You have to admit, though, the subject keeps coming up because he's often seen leaving casinos," the first guy said. *"There's also been talk about him being in debt to a bookie. Now*

how is that possible? He's one of the wealthiest sports figure out there. Yet, he owes money for gambling losses?"

They continued debating the issue, and the more they talked, the more frustrated Hunter got. This was why he limited how much he watched sports news or shows, but he'd turned the television on because of his publicist. She'd wanted him to hear what the sports world was saying about him lately. She was probably concerned that some of the crap they were saying was true. He would just have to show everyone that he didn't have a gambling problem.

He growled under his breath. He was so sick of this shit. What would he have to do to prove to them that he didn't have a gambling problem? He hadn't spent time on a casino floor since the day of Thomas's will reading.

Yet these guys were talking about him like they knew him. Like they'd gambled with him or something...

"You assholes don't know a damn thing about me," he mumbled through gritted teeth. "At least get your facts..."

He startled when Viviana touched his hand. He hadn't realized that she was awake.

"You okay?" she asked sleepily. "What's wrong?"

"Hey. Sorry I woke you," he said and scooted down in the bed. "Nothing's wrong. Just letting a couple of stupid sports commentators get to me."

He wrapped his arm around Viviana and pulled her close before kissing her.

"Mmm, what a way to wake up," she said, rubbing her hand against his stubbled cheek.

When they were together, he was usually clean-shaven, and he had planned to go back to that. But the night before, Viviana said that she liked the look, and he loved the feel of her hands on his face.

"I see you're still a morning person," she said on a yawn.

"Not like I used to be, but yeah, I still get up pretty early."

A smile spread across his mouth as he pushed hair away from her forehead and flattened some of the strands that were sticking up. Even with bed hair, she was still the most beautiful woman in the world.

"What time is it?" she asked, closing her eyes and snuggling into him. But before he could respond, her eyes popped open, and she bolted upright. "Oh, my goodness, Dannette is going to kill me. I didn't call and tell her I wasn't coming home. And your mom! What is she going to think? I need to get going." She started to get up, but Hunter stopped her.

The sheet had fallen to her waist, revealing her full, perky breasts—and just like that, he wanted her again. With her around, he practically stayed in a constant state of arousal. It had always been like that with her, and clearly that hadn't changed.

"Lay back down and relax," he said, and when she did, he eased the sheet back over her gorgeous body.

He couldn't wait to make love to her again, but no sense in tempting him anymore than he already was. Especially since he wanted to give her body a little more time to recover.

"Dannette knows you're still here," he said, gathering her into his arms again. "After you fell asleep, I called Scott, who she was still with, and told him to tell her. As for my mother... I'm not sure what she'll say. By now, she probably knows you're here, but..."

"Maybe I can sneak out the back," she said, and lifted her worried eyes to him.

Hunter almost laughed, but he didn't want to come across as insensitive. "You're not sneaking out the back. We're grown, and she knows how I feel about you. She's going to be thrilled that we're back together."

"Yeah, but..."

"No buts. Since it's Sunday and you're off today, how about if we get up, have some breakfast, then head to your place so that you can change clothes? If you don't have plans, I'd love for us to spend the day together and continue getting reacquainted...outside of the bedroom."

A slow, sweet smile spread across her face and Hunter's heart flipped inside of his chest.

With just a smile, she made him feel like everything was right in the world. They would never get back the years that they'd lost, but he was hopeful that they'd build on the love they had for each other. With what they'd been through, in the end, their relationship would be stronger than it had ever been.

Viviana was what he'd been missing in his life, and he was ready to move forward...with her.

"I'd like that," she said, "But I would still prefer to sneak out the back."

Hunter laughed and kissed the top of her head while hugging her.

Yep, we're going to be all right, he thought as he mentally planned how they'd spend their day.

Chapter Sixteen

Is it crazy to be madly in love with a man that I haven't seen or been with in seven years?

That's what Viviana asked herself as she watched Hunter sign a few autographs for fans. He had stepped away from the table so as to not have people standing over her. He had always been thoughtful where she was concerned, and she was glad that hadn't changed.

Viviana glanced down at the menu in her hands. They were currently at Buddy V's Ristorante in the Venetian, Hunter's favorite Vegas hotel. They'd spent the whole day together, roaming around Nevada like tourists, and getting to know each other again. They had both agreed that it wouldn't be realistic to think that they could pick up where they'd left off, but Viviana might've been wrong.

She and Hunter had a special bond; like they were created just for each other. She had always thought that, and with their reunion, she really believed it. Being with him felt as natural as it had the first time they'd met. Back then, they'd hit it off from day one and with each passing year, their relationship had blossomed.

Viviana glanced up as Hunter was trying to pull away from adoring fans. She couldn't much blame them. There was something about the man that drew people to him. It wasn't just his amazing skills on the basketball court, it was his charm and charisma that made him approachable and likable.

But many didn't get to see the other side of him—the side that could shut down his emotions or go off if pushed too far. Even though that never happened while they were together, Viviana was sure it would've happened if she would've tried talking to him after she'd left him. She could only imagine the turmoil that he'd gone through.

Hunter loved hard. If he cared about you, he was loyal to the end, but betray him, and he wanted nothing to do with you.

Thank God Hunter's giving me another chance.

She was so glad that Thomas was wrong about Hunter never forgiving her.

"I'm sorry, baby," he said, interrupting her thoughts when he returned to the table. "That won't happen again today."

"What's up, Hunter? Congratulations on the finals win, man," a fan said as he passed by the table.

"Thanks," Hunter said absently and returned his attention to Viviana. "I'm all yours for the rest of the day."

The server came and took their orders. Viviana requested the shrimp scampi, while Hunter ordered the grilled salmon.

"Do you ever get to go out without being bombarded by fans?" Viviana asked when the server walked away. Hunter had been making a name for himself while they were together, but now, his notoriety was on a different level. He was considered one of today's top ten players in the NBA.

"For the most part," he said, and explained that most people respected his personal space when he was out eating or when he was on a date. Of course, there were the exceptions—those who approached and didn't care if they were interrupting him. They'd still ask for an autograph or photo. Occasionally he'd relent and give them one, but other times, he wasn't afraid to say no."

"Or I'll have a couple of security guards shadow me and run interference, if necessary," he said as he sipped his beer. "When we leave here, I'll make sure we have a couple of people with us."

They talked about any and everything as they ate. This was what Viviana had missed. Well, at least *some* of what she missed. Their conversations had always flowed effortlessly, and now was no different. She enjoyed being with him in any capacity, and every minute that they were together was so special. Being with Thomas for the last seven years made her appreciate her time with Hunter even more.

"Let's talk about your living arrangement," Hunter said. "I have an idea to run by you."

Viviana looked at him warily as she savored her pasta. "I'm almost afraid to hear this idea."

He chuckled. "Why? You think you're the only one at the table who has brilliant ideas rolling around in your mind? I'll have you know, I have a few of my own."

"Really? Okay, let's hear the one about my living arrangement."

"I have a three-bedroom, three-bathroom luxury condo right off of the Strip. I rarely use it. Why don't you move into it?"

Viviana started shaking her head before he could finish his last sentence.

"Don't say no. You haven't even seen it."

Viviana *tsk*ed. "I'm not staying in some love shack that you've used over the years to bed your female companions. I know you had a life outside of me, but I know I wouldn't be comfortable knowing that—"

"I have never taken a woman to that place, I swear. I only use it when I'm in town gambling or hanging out with some buddies."

As far as she knew, Hunter had never lied to her, and she trusted he wasn't lying now. Still, it would be too weird moving into his place, especially when she could afford her own.

Then again, they agreed that they were going to move forward with the relationship. This setup could be a win-win, and it would also make her feel close to him while he traveled most of the year.

"I'll think about it," she said, her tone noncommittal.

"Okay, but I bet you'll love the place."

"Now, speaking of betting," Viviana said, effectively changing the subject. She'd been wondering how to bring this up. "I was surprised to hear about your gambling...situation."

She had heard a little of what the sports commentators were saying on the television when she woke up that morning. At the time, it hadn't seemed like a good idea to bring up the topic with Hunter. But it was a topic that couldn't be ignored... at least not if they wanted to move forward in their relationship.

After dealing with her mother's gambling over the years— actually, her mother's *everything*—Viviana didn't want to go through that again. That was assuming it was true what the media was saying about Hunter. She wanted to give him the benefit of the doubt. Still, it didn't matter how much she loved him—they couldn't be together if he had a gambling issue. That was a deal-breaker.

She could deal with his NBA travels and the amount of time they would be apart, but gambling—no way. Thanks partly to her mother's gambling addiction, Viviana's life had been turned upside-down. She couldn't go through anything like that again.

"I know you used to gamble recreationally," she said carefully, "but is it true about what the media is saying about you? That you have a gambling problem?"

Hunter sighed and picked at his vegetables.

"No, it's not true. Sure, over the last few years I've gambled and bet on games." He lifted his hands out in front of him. "Not NBA game, but other sports. I'm not addicted. And I'm not your mother," he said with a bite in his tone.

Viviana didn't say anything. She wanted to believe him, but...

"I'm sorry I snapped at you," he said before she could form her next thought. "You have every right to question me about anything, especially after what you've been through. It's just that I'm tired of defending myself with everyone. Yes, I enjoy gambling. It's like a sport to me, but I have it under control."

Viviana nodded. "I'm glad to hear that, and I had to ask. I want us to get back what we had, but I'll admit that I have a few trust issues. Between my mother and Thomas, I have a hard time not expecting the worst of people, but that's my problem."

"I get it," he said, staring into her eyes. "After you left, I couldn't let anyone get close. Even now, it scares the hell out of me."

Again, that guilt that wouldn't seem to leave her alone pierced her in the chest. She knew he forgave her, but how long would it take to forgive herself?

"I started gambling more after you left," Hunter admitted. "It was an outlet for me, though I didn't realize it at the time. It'll probably sound weird, but I haven't had the urge to place any wagers since you've been back. Yes, I know it's only been a couple of days, but I'm in Vegas, a playground of sorts for me, and I haven't done anything I usually do."

"I'm glad," she said.

He covered her hand with his on the table and squeezed. "I want what we used to have, Viviana. That includes trust. I know you trust me to a certain extent, but it's going to take time for both of us to get where we used to be. I really believe we can get there, though."

Viviana squeezed his hand back. "I think so, too, and that's what I want."

She loved hearing him admit that he wanted them to have a second chance at love. She wanted that more than she wanted anything else in the world. There was no doubt in her mind that Hunter was the only man for her.

We can do this.

They could have everything that she had destroyed when she felt she had no other choice but to walk away.

* * *

Once they were done eating, Hunter went back to their earlier conversation about her moving into his place. It was a great idea, and he knew she'd love it the moment she saw it. If he was honest, part of his suggestion was for selfish reasons. He wanted her in his space again, and right now, at this stage in their relationship, the condo idea was a good one.

When they were ready to leave, Hunter called his driver who also served as security whenever he was in town. He had already discussed with him and another security specialist that he might need them to shadow him and Viviana as the day went on.

Hunter hadn't been with Viviana in so long, he wanted to enjoy dating her all over again. The problem was, he didn't want more fans stopping him every few minutes for an autograph or a photo. He loved his fans and was fine with chatting it up with them, but sometimes he just wanted to be out and about with his woman without extra attention.

My woman.

It felt good to call Viviana his woman again. If he had his way, she would one day be his wife. But he wasn't going to rush what they were rebuilding. She had just gotten out of a bad marriage, and he wanted her to have time to recover from her life with Thomas.

"How about some gelato?" he asked as they strolled hand in hand through the halls of the Venetian. With his height and notoriety, it was hard to just blend in with his surroundings. People were staring and pointing, but at least they were keeping their distance.

"I temporarily forgot what it's like to be seen with you," Viviana said with a smile as they waited in line for their gelato. "Have you gotten tired of the attention yet?"

The attention must be bothering her. She'd mentioned the subject a couple of times in the last hour or so.

"It mainly bothers me when I'm with you or other members of my family," he whispered and brushed her bangs from her eyes. "You guys didn't sign on for this, and when I'm with any of you, I don't want to be bombarded by fans. But most of the time, I'm still all right with it."

When they received their dessert, Hunter found a quiet spot, hidden by some flowers and what looked to be fake trees. He wasn't sure, but they provided some privacy as they sat on a concrete bench.

They ate in silence for the first few minutes, until Hunter spotted some gelato on the edge of Viviana's mouth. Her tongue slipped out to swipe it away, but she missed a spot.

"Here, let me help you." He leaned down and kissed the area on the edge of her mouth, affectively licking up the gelato.

But there was no way he could be that close to her lips without getting a little taste of her sweetness.

Hunter wrapped his arm around her and pulled her against his body. He nibbled on her top lip, then her lower one before slipping his tongue into her mouth. Her sweetness mixed with gelato was almost too much to handle. He loved how she always gave herself freely to the passion of his kisses.

"Mmm, if you keep loving on my mouth like this, you're going to get something started," Viviana said when the kiss ended.

"Good. That's exactly what I'm aiming for." He stood and tossed both their empty containers in a nearby trash can. "Now, how about we get out of here and finish this somewhere a little more private, like the condo?"

Viviana let him pull her up, and she smiled. "I guess now is as good as time as ever to check out the place."

Chapter Seventeen

onday morning, Viviana headed to their suite of offices with pastries from a nearby bakery and a smile on her face. No doubt the extra pep in her steps hadn't gone unnoticed when she strolled through the employee entrance of the casino. She always smiled and said good morning, but today, she had even stopped and talked a few minutes.

And it had everything to do with her weekend with Hunter. God, she was crazy about that man. She hoped that the joy she was feeling would last forever, and it wasn't that temporary euphoria that people experienced when they first got into a new relationship.

"Good morning," Viviana said in a singsong voice when she walked into her office suite. She held up the bag of treats. "I brought breakfast."

"Well, someone is in a good mood," Dannette said from her desk. "I guess I don't have to ask what or who has put that smile on your face."

Viviana's cheeks heated. She hadn't been able to stop smiling in the last couple of days. Everything was so perfect that she feared that something would happen that would destroy her newfound happiness.

"How are you this morning?" Viviana asked and pulled the small white box from the bag.

"All is well for a Monday, but I have a feeling I'm not feeling as good as you are. You're actually glowing," she said on a whisper. There weren't many people in their area, but other employees were always stopping by. "I want to hear everything that happened after I left Hunter's rental the other night."

"I could say the same to you." Viviana sat in the chair next to the desk. They both sanitized their hands and then pulled cheese pastries from the box.

"I take it that you and Scott hit it off. You weren't home when I got in last night."

Dannette smiled wickedly. "He is such a sweetheart. I'm trying not to get my hopes or expectations up, especially with him being a basketball player. I'm sure he has a woman in every city, and I'm not trying to be another one. But I figured I'd have a good time with him while he's in town."

"Well, if it makes you feel better, Hunter said that he's a really good guy. Otherwise, he wouldn't have introduced you two. He also mentioned last night that Scott shot him a text and said that you're 'cool people.' So that's something."

Dannette laughed. "I'll take it, especially knowing that he can have any woman of his choice. Thanks for telling me. He was talking about heading back to LA tomorrow. I might see if I can convince him to stay a few more days."

"Can't hurt to ask," Viviana said, and popped the last piece of her breakfast into her mouth before standing.

"Wait, you can't get to work yet. You didn't tell me about your weekend."

Viviana smiled. Part of her wanted to keep her and Hunter's reunion to herself, but the other part of her wanted to tell Dannette everything. She wouldn't, though...but she'd give her the highlights.

"How about we order lunch in and catch up? Actually, we can compare notes," Viviana said, wiggling her eyebrows.

They both laughed and agreed on a time, then got to work.

* * *

Before Vivian realized it, the morning hours had flown by, and Dannette was walking in with their lunches.

"I hope you're hungry," she said as she set everything on the small round conference table that Viviana rarely used. She pulled out two large salads, Italian bread, two bottles of water, and oatmeal raisin cookies.

"You're right on time. I'm starving." Viviana sat at the table. It was nice to actually stop for a lunch break, something that she didn't do often enough. Normally, she worked straight through, snacking in between calls and meetings.

"Oh, before I forget," Dannette said as she started eating, "I saw on your calendar that you're taking off on Wednesday. Is that correct? I can't remember the last time you took a day off, especially in the middle of the week."

Viviana smiled. She couldn't remember the last time either, but Natasha, Hunter's sister-in-law, had called her a couple of hours ago. All of them—she and Hunter, along with Natasha, Alandra, and their spouses—were going to see John Legend perform on Saturday. Olivia and Wiz wouldn't be joining them since they had already returned to Chicago.

At first, Natasha wanted Viviana to recommend a good place for shopping. But then she asked if Viviana was free to go shopping with her and Alandra Wednesday.

Until the other day at the cookout, Viviana couldn't remember the last time she'd felt a part of a family. It had been a little overwhelming, yet thrilling at the same time. Now, she had an opportunity to go shopping with the women who had pulled her into their circle as if they'd known her forever. She actually had girlfriends, and she was totally thrilled. No way was she passing up the opportunity to go shopping with them, even if she really should be working.

"Yes, that's correct," Viviana finally said. "I'll be spending some time with Natasha and Alandra while they're in town."

Dannette grinned. "I'm so proud of you! You're finally doing something fun, instead of slaving away here in the office. It's about damn time. I love you, girl, and your incredible work ethic. But your work-life balance has been totally out of whack from the moment I met you."

Viviana laughed. "It really has, hasn't it? You're right; the last few days have been a lot of fun and it's made me realize what all I've been missing in my life."

"I'm so happy for you." Dannette gave Viviana a one-arm hug before sitting at the table next to her. "Speaking of Natasha and Alandra, can I just say that they are some total badasses? I've never met a female hospital chief of staff!"

Viviana narrowed her eyes at her friend. "Have you ever met any chief of staff?"

Dannette chuckled. "Well, no, but still...a female one? Girl, you know Tasha has to be a total badass to handle that type of responsibility. And don't even get me started about Alandra. The sister is *CIA*. She probably kicks ass and takes names. That is *mind-blowing*."

"Alandra *used* to work for the CIA," Viviana corrected, though she was impressed with the woman, too. She also learned that Alandra had a black belt in tae kwon do. She literally could kick ass.

"Now she does some consulting for a research firm in Chicago," Viviana explained. "Either way, it sounds like they've both lived an adventurous life, especially where their husbands are concerned."

"I bet. I've never been around Navy SEALS before," Dannette said between bites. "But if all of them look like Malik, Quinn, and Wiz, I might have to find me one." She laughed. "Those guys are huge, and you can tell they absolutely worship the ground their wives walk on. And they are seriously protective of them. Remember during flag football when Scott...no, I think it was Ricardo...grabbed Alandra's flag, but she lost her footing and tripped? The look Quinn gave Ricardo could've turned the man to ashes. I was scared for him."

Viviana laughed. She had noticed that. "Yeah, Quinn is a little intimidating. I think the only time I saw him smile was when he was either talking to or looking at his wife and son. He is a little intense."

"A little? The man is scary as hell, and so is Malik, but at least his sense of humor makes him a little more approachable," Dannette said. "Okay, enough about everyone else, what's up with you and that tall drink of water? I take it that you two have kissed and made up?"

"We have, and I know this is going to sound crazy, but I'm still in love with him."

Dannette's mouth dropped open. "Tell me you didn't use the 'L' word already. You're going to scare the poor guy away."

"I did, but not the way that you're thinking." Viviana vaguely remembered all that she'd told Hunter the other night when she was telling him about her life with Thomas. But she did remember telling him *I never stopped loving you.*

"What does that even mean?" Dannette asked, confusion showing in her eyes. "You either told him that you love him, or you didn't."

"It means in my heart, I'm still in love with him, and yeah, I sorta told him that. And according to him, the feelings are..." Her words trailed off when someone pounded on the outer office door.

Dannette grumbled as she stuffed another forkful of salad into her mouth. "I locked the door, hoping that we could get through lunch without any interruptions. Clearly, that's not happening. So, hold that thought. Let me get rid of whoever that is. I'll be right back."

Viviana continued eating as she debated on what more she could tell her friend. She trusted Dannette, but Viviana wasn't good at sharing all of her business, or feelings for that matter, with anyone. Except for with Hunter. He was such a part of her that talking with him was as natural as breathing.

Raised voices outside of Viviana's office door caught her attention, and she stopped eating.

"What in the world?" she mumbled and stood from the table.

"Move out of my way, little girl. I'm sure she will see me." The owner of the voice stormed into the room as if she had every right to do so, and Viviana stood frozen in place.

"I'm sorry, Viviana. I tried to stop her, but she forced her way in," Dannette said angrily. "And she says she's your...*mother?*"

Viviana stared at the woman who'd given birth to her. Chandra always looked good for her almost sixty years of life and that hadn't changed. As a matter of fact, she looked better than good, like a woman who has been well taken care of.

Instead of responding to Dannette's questioning gaze, Viviana said to Chandra, "How did you get past security?"

"I showed them my ID and told them I was your mother. We look alike. So, of course they let me up."

That was true. They looked enough alike that anyone would be able to tell that they were related. Their facial features and body types were very similar, down to the toned arms and legs. As for Chandra, both were on full display in her short off-the-shoulder light-blue dress that molded over her fit body.

The main difference in their appearance was their skin color and hairstyle. While Viviana was a dark mocha, Chandra had more of a sienna brown coloring. Their hair was also different. Viviana wore her natural curls and Chandra's hair was long and straight, hanging past her shoulders.

Yeah, her mother looked amazing, but Viviana could tell that she was still the same self-absorbed woman she had always been. It was in her dark, calculating eyes that were unwavering as she stared at Viviana.

Chandra might've thought that she could walk all over her the way she used to, but she had another think coming.

"What do you want?" Viviana asked with a bite in her tone. She wasn't happy to see Chandra, and there was no reason to pretend that she was.

"First of all, watch how you talk to me. I'm still your mother," Chandra said and strolled across the room to the desk in her four-inch strappy sandals. She sat in one of the guest chairs in front of the desk and crossed her legs. "Secondly, I need to talk to you...alone." She looked at Dannette dismissively.

Viviana wanted to tell Dannette to stay put, but she wasn't sure what Chandra was going to say. There was no need in letting her friend know just how much bad blood was between mother and daughter.

Viviana glanced at her friend and gave a little head nod toward the door. After a slight hesitation, Dannette walked out, closing the door behind her.

Instead of sitting at her desk, Viviana leaned against it and folded her arms across her chest. "I told you the last time I saw you that I was done with you, and that I never wanted to see you again. So, Chandra, what the hell do you want from me?"

Chapter Eighteen

Viviana asked the question, but she was almost sure she knew. Money. It was always about money when it came to her mother.

"I heard that Thomas died," Chandra said after a slight hesitation. "I'm sorry to hear that."

Viviana remained silent. There was no love between Chandra and Thomas, and she didn't believe the woman was sorry at all. As a matter of fact, she was surprised that her mother wasn't celebrating. If Viviana remembered correctly, Thomas had told her that he didn't want her in their lives.

"Thanks," Viviana said. "If that's all you came for, you can leave." Normally, she wasn't so rude, but when dealing with her mother, she couldn't help it.

Viviana's father had died when she was a toddler, and she'd had the misfortune of being raised by her mother, a woman who never loved her, at least by her actions. As a kid, Viviana didn't know that Chandra was the most selfish human being on the planet. But as she got older and had to endure many of her mother's poor choices, including homelessness, she learned pretty quickly how to take care of herself.

But up until the situation with Thomas, Viviana always tried to help her mother out whenever she got herself into a bind. They were each other's only family, and Chandra never let her forget it. She would always play the *family* card whenever she needed Viviana to bail her out, and it worked. Her mother was the world's best manipulator, and it took Viviana losing Hunter to realize just how much.

Since she was a little girl, Viviana had craved being a part of a family unit. She had finally got that when she and Hunter got together. Being around his mother made her realize just how much of a poor excuse for a mother she had.

And then Viviana had lost everything...thanks to Chandra.

"I've missed you," Chandra said with a straight face, and Viviana looked at her like she was crazy. Then she burst out laughing. It wasn't a humorous laugh. It was more like a *you-have-got-to-be-kidding me* laugh.

"Is that why you're here? Because you missed me? You do remember that you never gave a damn about me, right?" Anger stirred inside of Viviana, and she moved closer to the woman who she never understood. "You have made my life a living hell. So don't come up in here trying to act like you've forgotten what all went down between us. I care about you as much as I cared about Thomas—not at all. Now if you're done making a mockery of yourself, you can leave. I still don't want anything to do with you."

"Well," Chandra brushed invisible lint off of her dress, "I'm sorry you feel that way. But before I leave, we need to make arrangements."

Viviana narrowed her eyes at the woman. "What are you talking about? Arrangements for what?"

Chandra looked at her as if she'd lost her mind. "Don't play dumb. It's not a good look. I need you to continue paying me what Thomas was paying me. His clueless attorney acted like he didn't know anything about the financial arrangement between your husband and me."

Viviana just stared at Chandra. Surely, she wasn't hearing her correctly.

"What are you talking about? Why was Thomas paying you?"

"Stop playing dumb!" Chandra snapped. "You know he was paying me to stay away from *you*. He told me I was toxic or some crap like that." She waved the comment off. "Anyway, I held up my end of the deal, but he still owes me. I need my money, and since he's gone, I assumed you would take over the payments."

Viviana's mouth dropped open, and Thomas's words from his letter came to mind.

I protected you from more than you realize. But you're on your own now.

So that's what he meant. He figured since he was paying her mother to stay out of her life, he was protecting her.

"Pay up, baby." Chandra grinned.

"I'm not giving you a damn thing," Viviana seethed. "You worthless piece of—"

"Who the hell do you think you're talking to?" Chandra leaped from her seat and put her hands on her hips. "Just because you're living high off of Thomas's money doesn't give you the right to talk to me any type of way. If you don't pay me, my ass is going to be all up in your life. I'm sure that's something that neither one of us wants. Now, if you want the peace that you're probably accustomed to, I suggest we talk and come up with a monthly stipend that we can both live with."

"I thought you were crazy before," Viviana said, shocked by the nonsense she was hearing, "but now I know you've lost your mind. I'm not the gullible person I used to be. I don't give a damn about you or your wants. I can't stand being around you, but still, there is no way I'm paying you money...for *any* reason. Now get the hell out of my office!"

Chandra didn't move. Instead, she reclaimed her seat. "Not until we discuss my money."

Viviana walked back around her desk and pushed the red button on her phone. She kept her attention on Chandra in the process.

"Yes?" Dannette answered almost immediately.

"Get security up here ASAP," Viviana said. She watched as her mother's eyes widened.

"Already on it," Dannette responded, and the office door flew open.

Not only were there two of their biggest security guys strolling in, but Hunter walked in with them.

Chandra gasped at the sight of him. "What are you doing here? Surely, you're not..." Her gaze bounced between him and Viviana. "You two are back together?"

Viviana hadn't realized Hunter was in the building. Part of her wished he had stayed out of sight from her mother. The woman had caused him enough grief to last a lifetime. The last thing he needed was for her to start spreading lies again.

But the other part of Viviana was so happy he was there. Not that she couldn't fight her own battles. She just always felt a sense of calm whenever he was near. Before he walked in, she felt like she was going to blow a gasket. Now? She just wanted to fall into his arms and pretend her mother didn't exist.

"You okay?" Hunter asked, his gaze steady on her. Every time he looked at her like that, her heart turned over in response.

"Yeah, I'm fine. I just need her escorted off the premises."

He looked at Chandra for the first time since walking into

the office, and the disgust on his face matched what Viviana was feeling.

"So, you two are back together," Chandra said quietly. "Why? After what happened, I'd think—"

"Get her out of here," Hunter said to the guards. "And make sure she's banned from the casino as well as the hotel." After he spoke the words, he glanced at Viviana and gave her a look as if to ask, *is that okay?*

"I agree," she said. "My *mother* is not allowed anywhere on the premises. If she shows up at any time, call the authorities and have her arrested for trespassing."

"Let's go, ma'am," one of the security guards said.

"No, not until she hears me out and we have an agreement."

"Goodbye, Chandra," Viviana said.

When her mother wouldn't stand up, each security guard grabbed one of her arms and escorted her out. She was half their size. One of them could've carried her out of the room. Viviana assumed that the way they'd grasped and removed her had been some type of protocol.

The moment they left the office, Dannette closed the door, leaving Hunter in the office with Viviana. He pulled her into his arms, and she couldn't stop the tremor that shook her body.

"Are you sure you're okay?" Hunter asked with concern in his voice.

"I am now. What made you stop by?" she asked.

"Dannette. I was upstairs in my temporary office, and she happened to call. She said she wasn't sure what to do but explained that your mother was here and that the visit seemed a little tense. I told her to call security. I just happened to show up here at the same time they did."

Viviana leaned back and looked up at him. "I'm glad you're

here, but now that my mother knows you're back in my life, what if she goes to the media again?"

Hunter gave a slight shrug, then leaned down and kissed Viviana. His kiss was hot enough to melt metal, and she gripped the front of his shirt, deepening their connection.

Suddenly all was well in her world again.

She hadn't been kissed by many men, but no one kissed like Hunter. No one made her feel out of control with need the way he did, and no one ever would.

When they finally pulled apart, Hunter stared down into her eyes. "If Chandra tries to wreak havoc in our lives again, we'll deal with her...together. No more handling blackmailers on your own, and no more going off marrying anyone else to get her out of our lives. Understood?" he said the words seriously, but she didn't miss the humor in his eyes.

Viviana slapped a hand against his hard chest. "Fine! I won't run off and get married again." Thinking about her and her mother's conversation, Viviana huffed out a tired breath. "On a serious note, Hunter, I'm sure she's not going to go away quietly."

Viviana told him about the conversation that she'd had with Chandra, and the slight threat that her mother issued. She had no doubt that Chandra would keep showing up, but she wondered what the woman would do if Viviana continued to refuse to pay her.

"I'm not giving her a dime," she said, but deep down she wondered if it might be worth it to ensure keeping her out of their lives.

"Well, if she comes around again, we'll deal with her," Hunter said as he rubbed the back of his neck. "I'll give my publicist a heads-up just in case Chandra does start spreading lies again, but I don't think she will. She knows that that would be a definite way of never getting anything from either of us."

Viviana nodded. "Good point, and Thomas isn't around for her to go to him. She has burned so many bridges, her best bet is to play nice with me and hope that I change my mind. Which I won't."

"Good. I hated the way she used to use you." Hunter pulled her back against his body. "Now, how about another kiss?"

"For you? Anything."

Viviana lifted up on tiptoes and slipped her arms around his neck before covering his mouth with hers. She might've started the kiss, but Hunter quickly took over, and his demanding lips caressed hers.

God, she loved this man. As long as they stuck together, not even her mother could pull them apart again. And if she tried, Viviana was prepared to fight like hell to keep what she and Hunter were building. No way would she let Chandra Connelly come between them again.

Not now. Not ever.

Chapter Nineteen

"I know you two are going to find something here," Viviana said as she pulled up to her favorite boutique—Soledad's Closet. The owner, Soledad, was a sweet, older woman who had opened the store with her mother thirty-some years ago. Her mother had since passed away, and now Soledad and her daughter ran the business.

"Is this it to the right?" Alandra asked from the back seat. Viviana smiled as she glanced out the window. The white stucco building with black trim and black, pink, and white awnings was located on the corner. Some of the one-of-a-kind designs were displayed in the huge picture windows and drew people in easily.

"Yes, isn't it adorable? Wait until we get inside. They have crystal chandeliers, chaise lounges, and the one-on-one personal attention that the owners give will definitely make you a repeat customer. Actually, it's a mother-and-daughter team who run the place. You guys are going to love them."

"Can't wait," Alandra said as they all climbed out of the vehicle.

"Did you say that most of the items are one of a kind?" Natasha asked as they approached the building.

"Yes." Viviana pulled open the door open. "They make almost everything, and they have tailoring services right on site."

"Good afternoon, ladies. Welcome to Soledad's," Loretta greeted, then recognition showed in her eyes. "Oh, Viviana. Girl, welcome back. Mama was just saying that she hadn't seen you in a while."

"I know. Life has been so busy lately. I haven't done much shopping." Viviana accepted a hug from her. "But I'm here now, and I brought some friends with me."

She introduced the women, and for the next hour they hung out like old friends. Between trying on clothes, drinking tea, and chatting, Viviana was enjoying her time with the ladies. She and Dannette shopped together occasionally, but not like this. The few times they'd gone looking for clothes and shoes together, it was mall shopping.

They had bounced from one store to another, and Viviana quickly realized that she preferred a more intimate shopping experience, like what boutiques offered. It looked like Natasha and Alandra felt the same since they didn't seem to be in a hurry to leave.

"What do you think of this?" Natasha held up a mustard-colored jumpsuit that cinched at the waist.

"It's beautiful, and it looks amazing on you. Do you have shoes to go with it?" Viviana asked. She had already found a couple of outfits and was sitting near the dressing room where Natasha and Alandra were trying on clothes.

"I don't. Do you have time to do some shoe shopping?" she asked as she turned left and right in front of a full-length mirror.

"Sure. I took the whole day off."

"Did someone say shoes?" Loretta walked toward them carrying several shoe boxes. "These three-inch strappy sandals will go well with the jumpsuit, as well as the dress you decided on earlier. What size shoe do you wear?"

After another hour, they were finally checking out. Viviana had finished up before Alandra and Natasha, and she was staring out of the large window while she waited.

The store was located on a quiet street and the area had a small-town vibe. It definitely had walkability, but not many people were out and about, probably because it was a Wednesday afternoon.

Viviana straightened when a familiar person walked up to her car that was parked out front.

"What the..." She couldn't believe her eyes when she saw her mother peering inside the vehicle. "What is she doing here?" Viviana mumbled. She had a feeling that she'd see Chandra again, but not this soon. Without another thought, she headed to the door.

"Are you trying to leave us?" Alandra joked as she walked toward Viviana carrying a dress bag over her shoulder and a shopping bag that contained boxes of shoes.

Like Natasha, Alandra was a beautiful woman with a lithe body whose walk was graceful and fluid like a dancer. Dressed in a white halter top and fitted jeans with low-heel sandals, she looked more like a college student instead of a woman in her late thirties.

"No. I saw someone hanging around my car, and I was getting ready to go out and see what she wanted."

"Okay, I'll go out with you. Tasha, we'll meet you outside," Alandra called over her shoulder to her sister who was still at the counter paying for her items.

"All right, I'll be there in a second."

They walked out, and Chandra whirled around, looking guilty for being caught lurking around Viviana's car. Viviana popped the trunk as she walked to the back of the vehicle.

"What are you doing here, Chandra?"

She propped her hands onto her hips. "Is that any way to talk to your mother?"

"Your mother?" Alandra asked in surprise.

"In name only. She stopped being my mother a long time ago and until the other day, I haven't seen her in years." Viviana put her garment bag in the trunk and reached for Alandra's items.

"Can we chat in private over there for a minute?" Chandra asked and pointed to the side of the building. "I just want to talk. It won't take long." Her mother looked a little anxious, rocking from one foot to the other while glancing around.

Viviana wondered if she'd been drinking or if she was high. Either one wouldn't surprise her. Growing up, she didn't recall her mother using drugs, but she'd had plenty of drunken incidents.

"The doors are open," Viviana said to Alandra but handed her the key since she was getting ready to move away from the car. It had one of those push-button remotes to start the car, but the key needed to be near the vehicle.

Viviana started walking away with Chandra and couldn't help wondering how her mother knew where she'd be. Before she could ask, Natasha strolled out of the store, smiling.

"I love this place. I can see why it's one of your favorites," she said. "We definitely have to come back the next..." Her voice trailed off and her gaze darted between her and Chandra, who had already walked to the edge of the building. "Where you going?"

"Just going over here and see what my mother wants." She

frowned. "Your mother?" By her expression, Viviana assumed that Natasha had probably heard that there was no love between her and Chandra.

"Yeah. Alandra has the key. It'll only take a second. You guys can go ahead and get in."

Viviana hoped they got into the car because it was too hot out to be standing in the middle of the sidewalk. But considering the way she and Alandra were eyeing Chandra, they didn't trust her any more than Viviana did.

"How did you know where I was?" Viviana asked again when she approached her mother. "Are you following me?"

"Of course not. I was just walking by and thought that was your car. I wanted to..."

Unease clawed through Viviana, and now she was the one looking around. There was no way her mother knew what type of car she drove.

What is she up to?

Viviana started to back away, but before she could take two steps, a black van came out of nowhere and jumped the curb, almost hitting her.

"Oh, my God!" she yelped and jumped back.

Before she could process what was happening, two huge guys jumped out. Panic soared through her, and her fight-or-flight kicked in. She turned to run, but only made it as far as the front of the van before a man's strong arm grabbed her around the waist. He lifted her off the ground.

"Help!" she screamed at Alandra and Natasha. "Help!"

Her heart pounded hard against her chest and fear strangled her as she kicked out her legs and twisted in the man's hold while swinging her arms. She had to get away, but the person was too strong.

"Let me go!" she pleaded.

"Hey! Let her go!" Alandra yelled from behind them, and she either punched or kicked the guy because he fell forward.

"What the fu—" the man growled and dropped Viviana.

Her head barely missed the side of the van when she landed hard on her hands and knees. Pain shot through her arms and legs, but she jumped up in time to see Alandra kick the guy on the ground a second time.

"Ohmigod! Tasha!" Viviana said, when she realized Natasha was fighting the other man to keep him away from them, but she wasn't faring well. At least not until Alandra did some type of roundhouse kick, catching the guy on the side of the neck.

When he backed away from Natasha, the three of them took off running toward the car, but the van moved forward, blocking them from passing. Then one of the guys jerked her back.

"I don't want to kill you, but I will."

She turned to see the man who'd been fighting Natasha, and he had a gun in his hand. "Now, all of you, get in the van," the gunman said.

"Dude, what are you doing? He only wants—"

"We're taking all of them. Now move!" The gunman shoved Viviana forward toward the van.

Alandra and Tasha were behind her, but she didn't see them. Still one of them must've done something because the other guy growled, "Bitch!"

Viviana flinched when she heard a slap and one of the women cried out.

"Let them go," she said. "I don't know what this is about, but clearly, I'm the one you want. Just let them go."

"Shut up and get in," he said, pushing Viviana forward. When she got in the cargo van, she saw Chandra sitting on the bench seat.

"You did this?" Viviana growled.

She had a smug look on her face. "See, you should've just paid me. When I got a better offer, I took it."

Viviana didn't even feel herself move. Fury forced her forward and she grabbed Chandra by the hair and pulled her to the floor. She would've punched her, but one of the guys yanked on her arm and jerked her back.

"Knock it off, and get over there and sit down," he roared, shoving her across the van where she stumbled and fell onto the bench.

He tied her hands to a hook on the van, and the other men did the same to Alandra and Natasha, who were positioned on a bench in front of Viviana. That's when she saw the side of Alandra's face and her bloody lip.

The moment the men slammed the sliding door shut, Viviana said, "Are you okay?" The moment the words left her mouth, she realized it was a stupid question.

"Yeah, I'm fine." Alandra stared at Chandra. "So, this is your mother, huh?"

"I heard she was a piece of work, but to help kidnappers snatch you is lower than low," Natasha said. "They could've killed you. Hell, they could've killed all of us, and all she did was stand around and watch."

"Don't you sit over there all high and mighty. You don't know a damn thing about me," Chandra snapped. "Viviana had her chance to do right by me, but she didn't take it. That's on her."

Instead of giving a damn about Chandra, Viviana stared at Alandra and Natasha. Considering what they'd just gone through, the women were calmer than she would've expected. Maybe they were like her and freaking out on the inside because Viviana's heart was beating hard and fast enough to beat right out of her chest.

But Alandra and Natasha weren't breathing hard. They weren't sweating, and they didn't even look scared. It was as if they knew something she didn't know.

But what?

"Why are you back here?" Alandra asked Chandra. "Shouldn't you be up front with your cohorts?"

Viviana glanced at her mother, who looked as if she didn't have a care in the world, and the situation from seven years ago came rushing back. The hurt, the anger, and the disgust Viviana felt years ago when Thomas blackmailed her.

How could her own mother treat her with such disdain? What had she ever done to her to warrant so much hate? Because it had to be hate. What other reason could her mother have for not giving a damn about her?

"Never mind why I'm back here," Chandra said to Alandra, practically growling her response. "Who are you two?"

"Never mind who we are," Natasha said in the same tone that Chandra had just used.

"It's almost six o'clock," Alandra said, almost as if she was talking to herself. "I told Q I would be home by six. This isn't going to end well."

Viviana didn't know what the hell that meant, but it seemed to make Alandra even calmer. Viviana wanted so badly to ask what was going to happen if she wasn't home by six, but not with Chandra around.

Natasha must've been reading Viviana's mind, because she gave her a sympathetic look. "It's going to be okay," the woman said quietly.

How could she be so sure?

It repulsed her to look at her mother, but Viviana did anyway. "Who are the guys who grabbed us?"

Her mother was silent for so long and was inspecting her manicured nails. Viviana didn't think she would respond, but then Chandra said, "They work for Frankie. Seems your boyfriend...fiancé, or whatever the hell Hunter is to you, got on the bookie's bad side. Not a good move. I should know—been there. Now Frankie's going to use you to teach Hunter a lesson."

Ice clogged Viviana's veins at the mention of Hunter and a bookie. She didn't trust her mother any further than she could throw her, but deep down, Viviana knew she was telling the truth. And the mention of Frankie's name reminded her of the man she'd met at the club last week...the same time Hunter was there.

She glanced across the van at Alandra and Natasha, wondering how much they knew.

"Don't believe anything she says. Wait and talk to Hunter," Natasha insisted. "Don't jump to conclusions."

It was too late.

She already had.

Hunter had sworn that he wasn't gambling. That he didn't have the urge to do so since reuniting with her. Yet, here she was, suffering the consequences of his indiscretions.

A new wave of anger and hurt pulsed through her, and tears pricked the back of Viviana's eyes, but she refused to let them fall.

How could Hunter do this to her? He knew what she'd gone through with her mother. He knew that her mother's gambling had ruined Viviana's life.

Hell, it had ruined his life, too.

How could he get involved with a bookie and, in turn, put her in this type of situation?

Hunter gambling was a deal-breaker. She couldn't go through the heartache that came with being with...or loving a gambler.

Been there. Done that. I will not put myself through that again.

If she got out of this mess alive, she and Hunter were done.

Chapter Twenty

The smell of paint hit Hunter the moment he strolled into his new office at the casino. He stopped in the middle of the room and glanced around.

The interior designer had nailed his vision for the room. For the first time since learning about the casino inheritance, he felt at home.

A smile spread across his face as his gaze took in the light gray walls and mahogany office furniture. Everything looked upscale and perfect for the space, including the wall art that consisted of photos with him and some of NBA's greats—Michael Jordan, Lebron James, and there was even one with him and Dr. J. Then there was the carpet. The black and gray abstract made the whole room come together like a creative masterpiece.

The space felt like home—inviting and comfortable.

"This is cool," he mumbled and continued glancing around.

He hadn't planned on returning to the office this evening. He had received a voice message from the designer, requesting one last meeting tomorrow, and he agreed. But then she told him that the room was complete, and like a kid on Christmas Eve, he couldn't wait until tomorrow.

The office used to belong to Thomas, but Hunter wanted no trace of his brother in the place. He had hired the interior designer the day after he'd first met with Viviana about the partnership and next steps. He was glad he had. The obscene amount of money that he had paid to gut the office and put it back together within seven days was worth every penny.

Especially since they had finished ahead of schedule.

"What do you think, Mr. Graham?" his new assistant, Tonya, asked when he walked in.

That was another thing he had changed. Thomas's assistant had been moved to a different department with a new job title and slightly different responsibilities. She was happy about the move, and Hunter was glad to get his own assistant.

All of that was thanks to Viviana.

The more Hunter learned about his stepbrother's betrayal, the more he wanted to distance himself from anything part of Thomas. Except for Viviana, of course.

Funny how just a few days could totally change his mind-set. He thought he had lost her for good to his brother. Then they were thrown back together out of the blue, and once again, Hunter couldn't imagine his life without her.

She was always mine.

And he was prepared to do anything to keep it that way.

"I think it came out great, Tonya," Hunter finally said, "But I thought we were going to be on a first-name basis?"

"Oops, you're right. First name it is." She laughed, and her light blue eyes glimmered with amusement.

Tonya was in her mid-to-late forties and had been with the accounting department of the company for eight years. She'd told Viviana she wanted a change. So far, she and Hunter got along great. He thought she was overqualified and that she might get bored, especially since he wouldn't be in the office much. But Viviana assured him that Tonya would be the perfect fit. Her responsibilities were still being worked out, but in her previous position, she had been described as efficient, careful with personal information, loyal, and very knowledgeable about the company and its processes.

That was exactly what Hunter needed, especially when he started taking on more responsibilities in the future.

"Well, unless you need anything, I'm going to head out for the day," she said.

"Nope, I'm good, I plan on leaving in a few minutes, too."

She gave a slight nod. "Okay, have a good evening, and I'll see you tomorrow."

The moment she walked out of the room, Hunter's cell phone ring. He pulled the device from the front pocket of his jeans and glanced at the screen.

"What's up, bro?" he said to Malik. He had just seen him at the house and was surprised he was calling.

"Have you talked to Viviana lately?" his brother asked in a rush, sounding all businesslike.

Unease crept through Hunter. "Not for a few hours. She said her and the ladies were heading to some boutique, but I haven't—"

"They were supposed to be back by six," Malik snapped, and Hunter could hear Quinn in the background.

Hunter glanced at his watch. "Dude, it's only six-twenty. They probably ran into traffic or something. Just chill."

"Listen, asshole, Tasha's not answering her phone, and neither is Alandra. That doesn't happen, especially where Alandra is concerned. She and Quinn have a...system, for lack of a better word. If she was going to be late, she would call."

Hunter knew that Alandra had gone through hell years ago,

almost dying twice at the hands of a madman. Quinn hadn't fared much better and was crazy-protective of her.

Hunter also knew that his brother was worried about Tasha. Both men had reason to be concerned about their women. "Call Viviana. See if you can reach her. Hopefully, we're concerned for nothing."

"Okay, I'll...wait, don't you guys have some way of tracking them?" Hunter asked. After the shit that they'd all been through, Wiz, who was a tech genius, had created some type of tracking device. All of their women had a piece of jewelry that held the device.

Maybe I should get something like that for Viviana. I wonder what she'd think about me being able to track her moves.

"We do, but I try not to use it unless there's an emergency. I'll give it five more minutes before I get Wiz involved. But Quinn is not as patient as I am."

Hunter laughed. His brother didn't have a lick of patience.

So that was saying a lot about Quinn.

"Let me call Vivi, and I'll call you back."

When Hunter got her voicemail, that unease from a moment ago returned. He hoped they were all right, but the fact that none of them were picking up wasn't a good sign.

Especially if they were expected home by now.

Hunter left a message. "Hey, baby. Just checking on you. Call me as soon as you get this message and have Tasha call Malik. Talk to you soon."

He started to call Malik back, but his phone rang.

"Oh, good," he said, thinking that it was Viviana returning his call. A look at the screen, though, and he realized it wasn't her.

It was Frankie.

What the hell does he want?

Hunter didn't bother answering. He hadn't placed any

wagers with the guy, and as far as he was concerned, they were done. Frankie had no reason to be calling him.

Hunter meant what he told Viviana. Since she came back into his life, he had no desire to gamble or place bets, meaning he wasn't addicted like the media was claiming. He knew he could stop gambling whenever he wanted to.

At the time, he just hadn't wanted to.

His phone rang again, and Frankie's name flashed across the screen again. Now Hunter was curious about why the bookie would be calling him.

"Yeah," he said by way of greeting.

"I'm surprised you picked up. I figured I'd be the last person you'd want to talk to," Frankie said on a chuckle.

"What do you want?" Hunter growled. "You have your money. What possible reason could you have for calling me?"

"Surely, you didn't think that I'd let you fuck with me and get away with it, did you?" the bookie said. "What would my other customers think if they found out?"

Hunter frowned. "What are you talking about? You got what was owed to you. Now leave me the hell alone."

"Oh, yeah, I got what I wanted and a little bit more," Frankie said. There was rustling through the phone line as if he was moving around. Hunter started to hang up, but Frankie started talking again. "I have something of yours that you might want back. Instead of me telling you what that is, check your text messages."

"Frankie, I don't have time..." Silence filled the phone.

"Hello?" Hunter said, then glanced at the screen and realized the asshole had hung up, and there was a text message.

What the hell type of game was this asshole playing?

When Hunter opened the text, there was a video and he pushed play.

"What the..."

Viviana's face appeared on the screen, and Hunter's heart slammed against his chest. Fear like nothing he had ever experienced before gripped his body.

No. No. No. God. No.

He covered his mouth with his hand as the video panned out, showing that she was in some type of vacant warehouse. Viviana was gagged and tied to a chair, twisting and turning, struggling to get loose. Her eyes were wild with fear, and Hunter's pulse amped up. His mood veered sharply to anger as he gripped his phone tight enough to shatter it.

"I'm going to kill him," he seethed.

He continued watching the video, and next to Viviana were Natasha and Alandra. Both women were tied up and gagged. Hunter brought the phone closer and that was when he saw Alandra's face.

"Oh, *shit...*" The other two women didn't appear to have bruises, but her cheek was bruised, and her lip was busted.

Son of a bitch. Quinn was going to be out for blood, and someone was going to die.

Hunter redialed Frankie, and he paced the room, waiting for the asshole to pick up. When his call went unanswered, he dialed him again. Finally, the bookie answered.

"I guess you know that I have something of yours and her friends," he said smugly.

"Motherfucker, you have gone way too far!" Hunter barked into the phone. "This has nothing to do with her or the others. Your issue is with me, not them. Now where the hell are they?"

"You fucked with me and my money, now I'm going to fuck with you. I'll return your girl when I'm good and ready."

Silence filled the line.

"Hello? Frankie?" Hunter yelled. "Dammit!" He lifted his phone to throw it across the office, but stopped himself just in time.

He called Frankie back, surprised when he answered.

"It doesn't feel good when someone has something of yours, does it?" Frankie chuckled, the sound grating over Hunter's skin like nails across a chalkboard.

Struggling to control his temper, Hunter took a couple of deep breaths before saying, "Where is she?"

"You want her, come get her, but you better come alone. I'll text you the address. If your asshole brother comes with you, she's dead and so are her friends." Frankie hung up.

Seconds later, a text came through with an address.

Hunter dialed his brother and rushed out of the office with the phone to his ear. He was going to get his baby, but he sure as hell wasn't going alone.

Chapter Twenty-One

"I'm taking off the bandannas, but if either one of you screams, they go back on. Understand?" Bryce, Frankie's lackey, said.

Viviana nodded. Out of the three men in the warehouse, Bryce was the one who seemed like he didn't want to be there. Like he wasn't really on board with the kidnapping, but still, he played a hand in snatching them off the street.

She had learned all of their names after being tied up for what felt like hours, but probably wasn't that long. Based on the large windows toward the ceiling, it was still daylight outside, but the sun appeared to be setting soon.

Bryce walked away and strolled toward the small room about thirty feet away. That's where Frankie, Keith, and Chandra were hanging out.

They had been arguing earlier; she heard them. Frankie hadn't liked that Keith had grabbed all three of them off the street instead of just her. But now they seemed to have settled down.

Either that, or they were arguing quietly where Viviana couldn't hear them.

She still couldn't believe that her mother played a role in having her kidnapped. But why should she be surprised? Chandra had disappointed her over and over, and proved that she didn't give a damn about her.

Viviana was going to do everything in her power to make her mother pay. She didn't know how yet, but she would definitely think of something because this...this was unforgivable.

Bryce went into the back room, and it was the first time that Viviana had a chance to talk freely with Natasha and Alandra.

"I am so sorry," she whispered, and guilt stabbed her in the chest. "I had no idea that my mother was setting me up. I swear."

"We know," Natasha whispered back. "Malik told me a little about what you and Hunter have been through with her. Which was why Lan and I didn't get in the car while you two were talking."

"I didn't know the story with her, but I didn't trust your mother from the jump. She looked shady," Alandra said.

Viviana was still trying to free her hands, which were tied behind her back. Her shoulders ached from the way they'd yanked on her arms, pulling them behind her to restrain her. At least her ankles were free, unlike Alandra's. The men had also added restraints to her ankles, tying them to the chair because they were afraid she'd start kicking them again.

"I hate that you guys got pulled you into whatever mess this is. I'm so sorry."

"Stop worrying. We're going to be fine, and we're going to get out of here," Natasha said. She wasn't as calm as she'd been in the van, but she still wasn't freaking out the way Viviana was.

"How can you be so sure? None of us have our purses,

phones, or any type of weapon that we can use on them," Viviana said, trying to keep her voice down but fear swirled inside of her. She kept glancing back at the small room to make sure their kidnappers were still in there. "How are we going to get out of here?"

"Well, first of all, Alandra *is* a weapon," Natasha said with a slight smile. "I'm pretty sure she can get out of the restraints."

Alandra grunted. "I think I can, but it's going to take a minute," she whispered, still struggling to get loose.

This was the first time the three women had been left alone since they'd been dragged into the warehouse, and Viviana wondered what was going on.

Frankie seemed a little more anxious than he was when they first arrived. Then he had been smug, acting like he had accomplished the greatest feat ever.

Viviana had learned a little about the situation. Though she was angry at Hunter for getting her wrapped up in his mess, she understood that Frankie's beef with him was from before she and Hunter got back together. What she didn't understand was why Hunter didn't pay what he'd owed right from the jump, but she planned to find out.

As for how Chandra located her, that was Keith's doing. Apparently, he had managed to track Viviana's car, but because she hadn't been driving much, there hadn't been an opportunity to snatch her.

That was where Chandra came in. Somehow, she and Frankie connected, and they had decided they could work together. But since arriving, Chandra hadn't been too happy. Viviana heard her tell Frankie that she wasn't leaving until he paid her what he'd promised.

Viviana sighed. Her sorry excuse for a mother had sold her out and thought nothing of it.

"Stop worrying. Malik is going to find us," Natasha said quietly.

Viviana frowned at her. "How? He can't track our phones. None of us have them."

"I have a tracking device in my diamond stud earrings," she said, turning her head slightly to move her hair away from one of her ears. That's when Viviana saw the glittering stones in the second hole in her friend's earlobe. She hadn't even realized Natasha's ears were double-pierced.

"And mine is in my wedding band," Alandra said quietly, lifting her arms up and down and trying to cut the plastic restraints against the chair.

Viviana just stared at the two women. They were some of the most unique women she'd ever met, and this bit of information intrigued her.

"Why?" was all she could say.

Alandra chuckled. "Girl, it'll take us a long time to explain the why, but trust me when I say my husband will find us. He has saved my life more than once, and I have no doubt he is on his way."

"But Viviana, brace yourself. Once Quinn sees that bruise on her face, there's going to be bloodshed, if not worse," Natasha said seriously, and Viviana shivered at the thought.

Hunter had told her that Quinn was not only a former Navy SEAL, but he was a part of black ops for the government. Quinn and Alandra had to live outside of the country for years for fear that enemies he'd made during his career would come after them. They had only recently returned to the Chicago area.

Part of her wanted to know their story, but the other part of her thought it might not be safe to ask.

They all stopped talking when the others reentered the open space.

"Frankie, you better pay me because I'm not leaving until you do," Chandra snapped.

With the speed of lightning, Frankie backhanded her, and sent Chandra crashing to the floor.

Viviana gasped, then clamped her mouth shut. If her hands hadn't been tied up, she might've even clapped.

"You are in no position to demand anything from me," Frankie growled. He jabbed his finger toward Chandra. Her eyes were wide with shock as she looked at him with her hand on her cheek. "I suggest you shut the hell up. I told you I'll pay you when the last part of this plan is complete."

The last part of the plan?

Viviana wanted to know what that was. When she looked at Alandra and Natasha, neither of them looked as confident as they had a moment ago.

God, please don't let us die in here.

"You know what? I'm not doing this," Bryce said. "I'm out."

"You walk out of that door, and we're done!" Frankie yelled after him, but Bryce kept walking back toward the room that they had just left. Instead of entering the room, he strolled out of a back door that Viviana hadn't noticed before.

"Good riddance," Frankie mumbled, and approached the women.

He stopped in front of Viviana, and she forced herself to look him in the eyes. No way was she going to show fear to this piece of trash.

"As long as your boyfriend shows up...alone...you'll live to see tomorrow. But let me tell you now, I don't care if you live or die. All I want is to make him pay for making a fool of me."

Viviana swallowed hard. She didn't know what he meant about making Hunter pay. She just hoped he didn't hurt him.

Better yet, she hoped that Natasha and Alandra were right, and that their husbands would show up.

"He's here," Keith said, strolling toward the far end of the warehouse to a hallway that led outside.

As he walked away, Viviana noticed the gun sticking out of the back of the waistband of his pants, and her pulse amped up.

The *he* had to be Hunter, but she prayed to God that he hadn't come alone. He wasn't a fighter. He was a basketball player, and she had a feeling that these guys had no intention of just talking to him.

A prickle at the back of her neck told her Hunter was there before she even saw him. From where she was sitting, she couldn't see the door, but she knew it was him.

"Where the hell is she?" Hunter roared, and Viviana bit down on her lip to keep the tears at bay. She was happy that he had come for her, but she was scared to death that he was going to get himself killed.

Keith shoved Hunter into the warehouse, and he stumbled forward. Viviana screamed before she could stop herself.

Oh, God, please...

Hunter had righted himself before he hit the floor, and he whirled around, catching Keith off guard when he slammed his fist into the side of the man's face.

Shock rolled through Viviana when Keith crashed against the wall, clearly dazed from the punch.

"Put your hands on me again, and I will *kill* you!" Hunter roared. He said the words with so much conviction, Viviana believed him. "Now where's my woman?"

He moved further into the area where they were being held, but then Keith charged toward him. Viviana opened her mouth to tell him to warn him, but Frankie yelled first.

"Keith, knock it off! He's mine!"

Viviana's heart was beating so hard and fast, she was sure it was going to leap out of her chest.

Where's Malik and Quinn? Hunter can't handle these two on his own.

"Once again, you clearly don't know who you're dealing with," Frankie said as Hunter moved closer. "You don't come up in here acting like you own this place."

"Frankie, I'm not doing this with you," Hunter said, making eye contact with Viviana before turning his attention back to the bookie. "I'm here. I'm the one you want. Now let them go."

"I'll let them go when I'm ready to let them go." Frankie pointed the gun at Hunter's head, and Viviana couldn't stop the whimper that slipped through. "Get over there," the bookie said, waving the gun to move Hunter forward.

"Baby, I am so sorry," Hunter said when he got closer. "Are you okay?" he asked, glancing at each one of them as he moved within arm's reach of Viviana.

"Stop right there," Keith ground out.

It was clear that there was bad blood between him and Hunter. He was as tall as Hunter and wider, but the fierceness that Viviana saw on her man's face told her that he was ready for a fight.

But Viviana hoped he wouldn't start one, especially considering the way he was holding his right hand close to his body. He must have hurt it when he punched Keith.

"Come on, Keith, man. This has nothing to do with these women. You guys want me, and here I am. Just let them go."

Chandra came forward, and Hunter's brows dipped into a frown.

"What the hell are you doing here?" he barked out, then looked at Viviana.

"She was in on it," Viviana said.

Keith turned to her. "Shut up!"

"Hey!" Hunter roared and stepped forward, but before he

could take another step, glass shattered, and Keith crumpled to the ground.

Viviana screamed when she saw blood smeared across the area near his head. Someone else had screamed, too, but she wasn't sure who.

Ohmigod. Ohmigod. Ohmigod. What is happening?

"What the..." Frankie yelled, but before he could lift the gun in his hand, a bullet slammed into his chest, and Viviana screamed again as he fell backward.

She was shaking so hard her chair was rocking.

"Shh...shh... It's okay, baby. Don't look," Hunter said in a rush and pulled out a knife to cut her restraints. "We gotta hurry and get out of here."

"Oh, my God. Are they..." Viviana couldn't even finish her sentence. She couldn't believe what had just happened.

In her state of shock, Viviana hadn't processed others were still screaming.

Chandra.

Chandra was the other one screaming as she started backing away from the group.

"Stop right there!" Hunter yelled at her, and she did. "Now get over here."

The next few minutes were like a blur as Malik and Quinn stormed in with their faces covered with bandannas and aviator shades covering their eyes.

Viviana's head was spinning as she tried to process what she had just witnessed.

"Sweetheart..." Hunter shook her and when she turned to him, he looked as if he'd been trying to get her attention for a while. "I need you to stay with me, all right? Can you walk?"

Viviana gave him a jerky nod, even though she wasn't sure.

"We gotta move," Malik said in a rush as he undid Natasha's restraints, and Quinn took care of Alandra.

"I ought to shoot his ass again," Quinn growled.

Viviana didn't hear the rest because Hunter was helping her stand up. He held her close to his body, then addressed Chandra.

"I suggest you get out of here," he told her. "The cops are going to be all over this place in a few minutes."

Tears and mascara were streaming down Chandra's face. "I —I don't know where to go," she stammered, and real fear showed on her face.

"I don't give a damn where you go," Hunter snapped. "But if you speak a word of this or come anywhere near Viviana again, you're dead. Do you understand? I need you to stay the hell out of our lives...or else!"

Her mother nodded nervously as she backed away from them. Then she turned and hurried out the door that Hunter had entered.

Hunter cupped Viviana's face and searched her eyes. "I know this is all crazy, but I promise to explain everything to you later. Right now, I just need you to trust us." He placed a kiss on her lips. "Okay?"

Viviana nodded. "I trust you," she said without hesitation.

She didn't understand what had just happened, or how they were going to clean up this mess, but she trusted him more than she had ever trusted anyone in her life.

"I trust you," she said again, and he swept her up into his arms.

"Good. Let's get out of here."

Chapter Twenty-Two

Hours later, Hunter sat in the kitchen of his rental home, staring out the window into the darkness. That's how he felt inside—dark. How else could he feel? He had almost gotten the people he loved killed, and for what? A damn gambling debt...and pride.

Stupid ass.

He would never be able to forgive himself for holding out on paying Frankie. It didn't make sense then, and it definitely didn't make sense now. His pride and arrogance had put too many people at risk.

Stupid ass.

He sipped from his glass of bourbon. It was the middle of the night, and the house was quiet with everyone asleep... except for him. He might never sleep again because the events at the warehouse kept playing over and over in his head.

After getting the call from Frankie, saying that he had Viviana, Hunter had been on autopilot. He feared the man would kill her.

Just the thought of that gutted Hunter. It was because of him that she'd even been put in danger.

He shook his head and slammed back the rest of the bourbon in the glass, then poured himself another. The liquor was strong, but so far it wasn't strong enough to dull the ache in his chest...in his heart.

If it hadn't been for Malik and Quinn, he didn't know what he would've done.

I probably would've gotten myself killed.

He'd known that Frankie was a loose cannon, but he had no idea he was capable of kidnapping...and even murder.

After the encounter with him at the club, Malik had looked into the bookie. There'd been a warrant out for his arrest in California, which was probably why he was in Vegas in the first place. Frankie had been under investigation for two murders in the last three years. There had never been enough to charge him with anything, but according to Malik's sources, the bookie had been responsible for both.

Now, knowing that, Hunter realized how lucky he was. He knew Frankie wasn't necessarily a man to play with, but he had no idea the man was capable of murder.

That thought—and knowing that Frankie could have taken out Viviana—sent a shiver through Hunter's body.

She could've been killed...and it would've been his fault.

After getting the call from Frankie earlier, telling him that he had Viviana, Hunter had met up with Quinn and Malik. They had already found the location of the warehouse and put together a plan to get the women out.

Hunter had feared for everyone's life, but he knew that Malik and Quinn were professionals. Personal security was their specialty, and getting bad guys was their passion. He'd known Quinn had been a part of black op teams, but he hadn't remembered that he was a sniper. With his security firm, Malik was well connected around the country, and Quinn's reach was even further. They'd both made a few calls and before Hunter knew it, not only did they have a plan, but they had weapons.

He shook his head and sipped his drink, cringing at the burn as the liquor slid down his throat. It was bad enough that he'd been stupid in screwing around with the bookie in the first place, but to pull Viviana into the mess...now, *that* was unforgiveable.

He loved that woman more than he ever thought he could love someone who wasn't his mother. Knowing that he'd put her life in danger gutted him.

She might've been upstairs sleeping in his bed, but he had no idea if he had destroyed everything that they'd started rebuilding. How the hell were they going to be able to move on from this?

"I can hear you thinking all the way upstairs," Malik said when he walked into the kitchen. Considering it was the middle of the night, and he had killed someone hours ago, he looked as if he didn't have a care in the world.

"How do you do it?" Hunter asked.

He watched as his brother grabbed a glass out of the cabinet, and potato chips out of the pantry. Then Malik joined him at the table.

"How do you do what you guys did tonight and live with it?"

"I can live with any of my decisions and actions if what I've done was to protect my family or innocent people," he said simply, and poured bourbon into his glass. "I have no regrets where this evening is concerned. We saved our women. As a bonus, we got rid of two lowlife motherfuckers who have caused more harm in this city than good."

Well, damn. When he put it that way...

"You fucked up," Malik said. "Your cockiness when

dealing with Frankie and the money you owed him was just stupid. If I find out that you've bet on anything ever again, even a fucking golf game, I'm going to kill you myself. I'm serious. For Mom's sake, I'll make it look like an accident, but I'll take your ass out of this world faster than you entered it. You feel me?"

Hunter nodded. He had already decided that he would never gamble again in his life. He had too much to lose.

Hell, he might've already lost the one woman who meant everything to him.

"Got it," he said. "I messed up big-time, and I don't know if Viviana is going to forgive me."

"She already has. Otherwise, she wouldn't be upstairs in your bed. Trust me when I say that I know what I'm talking about. Tasha has taught me well. You'll probably have to kiss Viviana's ass for the rest of your life, but she's not going anywhere if you do right by her."

A slow smile spread across Hunter's face. He was more than willing to kiss her fine ass, but he hoped his brother was right.

Hunter knew her well enough to know that if she was done with him, she wouldn't be there. But he was concerned that she was only there out of fear.

"I guess I'll soon find out," he said.

"Oh, and before I forget, you and Viviana won't have any more problems out of Chandra," Malik said, and stuffed a handful of chips into his mouth.

Hunter sighed and ran his hands down his face. "Is she still alive?"

"Yep. Quinn paid her a visit a couple of hours ago. He wanted to make sure she understood what would happen if she repeated any part of what took place today. When she agreed, I made a call. I know a guy."

Hunter chuckled. *Of course he did.* The man had connections that Hunter could only dream about.

"As of this weekend, she'll be living in New Jersey. She has a place to stay, a few dollars in the bank, and over the next few days, she's going to meet a guy and eventually fall in love with him."

Hunter stared at Malik to see if he was joking, and when he realized that he wasn't, Hunter burst out laughing. His brother never ceased to amaze him, and he always accomplished what he set out to do or have. If he said Chandra was going to fall in love and live happily ever after—it was going to happen.

A cell phone rang, and Hunter knew it wasn't his. He glanced at Malik, who dug his phone out of the pocket of his sweatpants.

"Yeah," his brother said when he answered. He didn't speak for a few seconds then disconnected the call.

"What was that all about?" Hunter asked.

"Grab that remote and turn on the TV. Turn it to a news station," Malik said, and went back to eating chips.

Hunter did as he was told.

Breaking News scrolled at the bottom of the screen and in the background was a smoldering frame of a building. The flames had completely demolished the structure, but still, Hunter recognized it immediately.

It was the warehouse.

He sat up straighter and turned up the volume.

"Authorities are saying that two bodies were found inside. One was burned beyond recognition and dental records will be needed to identify it. With the other, authorities have identified him as Franklin Evans, a known bookie here in the Nevada area as well as California. We have learned that Mr. Evans was a person of interest in a recent murder, and authorities believe that his death is tied to that case. They are also

saying that this was definitely arson. It's still early in the investigation but stay tuned for more information as the case unfolds."

"Please tell me that this can't be traced back to us?"

Hunter's head whipped around to find Viviana standing near the counter. She was wearing a baggy T-shirt and black leggings that she had borrowed from Alandra. Her face was scrubbed clean of all makeup and her hair was covered with a scarf, and yet she was still the most beautiful woman he had ever laid eyes on.

But the concern and the vulnerability in her eyes made his heart hurt, and all of his protective instincts kicked into gear.

He leaped from his seat. "Hey, baby, what are you doing up?"

He wrapped his arms around her, and hope swelled in his chest when she leaned into him and held on tightly.

God, he loved this woman. He didn't know what it would take, but he planned to spend the rest of his life showing her just how much.

"Please, just tell me." She pointed at the television. "Tell me that none of that will lead back to us."

"It won't," Malik said. "There is no way this can be tied to any of us. We made sure of that. Frankie was a bad guy who had more enemies than friends. Trust me when I tell you the authorities in Vegas and LA are going to be thrilled that he's off the streets. You have nothing to worry about."

Viviana nodded and laid her head against Hunter's chest.

"Good," she said. "That's good."

Malik left them alone in the kitchen, and Hunter knew he needed to say something to Viviana. He had to know that he hadn't screwed up a future with her.

He turned her to face him.

"Listen, I will never be able to express just how sorry I am for how things went down today. I never meant to put you in danger. I hope…"

"I forgive you," she interrupted. "I was angry at you when we were kidnapped, but thanks to Natasha, who went to bat for you, I know that the mess with Frankie happened before I came along. Besides, I know you would never intentionally put me in danger. I can say that with confidence. As for you and me… we're good. It's going to take me some time to mentally and emotionally recover from what happened today, but that doesn't change how much I love you."

Hunter leaned down and cupped her face, then kissed her. "I love you too, baby. God, I love you so much. I thought I had lost you, and I know I wouldn't have been able to recover a second time."

"You're not going to lose me." She lifted up on tiptoes and kissed him. "I'm in this for the long haul."

"Good, because I'm *never* letting you go."

Hunter gathered her into his arms and kissed her with everything in him. He meant every word he'd told her. He was never letting her go and planned to give her the life he'd wanted to give her seven years ago.

This time, he was playing for keeps.

Epilogue

O ne year later...

Viviana rode in silence in the back seat of a Chevy Suburban with dark, tinted windows. She never knew she could be as happy as she was in that moment.

The last year had been a whirlwind, full of unbelievable moments, both good and bad.

After Thomas died, she hadn't known what to expect. All she knew was that she was free. Free to live the life she had always dreamed of living.

But since then, her life had exceeded all expectations. Never in a million years could she have dreamed this big. She was living proof that anything was possible.

The weeks that followed the incident with Frankie had been emotionally tough. She hadn't felt guilty about his death, but processing how everything went down had been hard. Law enforcement never contacted them, and she and the others were never connected to the incident. For that, Viviana was grateful.

But after that whole situation, she did something she should've done years ago—she got counseling. From her childhood to her marriage to Thomas, there had been a lot of built-up guilt, anger, and even anxiety. After months of therapy, she'd felt like a new woman...a new human being. And during the process, she'd gained all the tools needed to start living her best life.

Now here she was, starting the next chapter.

Viviana sat up straighter when the driver drove through the gate and onto her and Hunter's new property. A smile spread across her face and a giggle bubbled inside of her.

Nope, never in a million years could I have dreamed that this would be my life...

The driver stopped the vehicle in front of the mansion.

"Home sweet home," Hunter said and climbed out of the vehicle. He jogged around to the other side and opened the door for her.

As they strolled up the cobblestone walkway, Viviana looked at the house as if seeing it for the first time.

It wasn't. It was the same home that Hunter had rented a year ago.

Now they owned it.

It was amazing what could happen in a year. Not only did they own the home, but they were also the official owners of the hotel and casino. They had even renamed it—The Majestic Grande.

Hunter had also retired from the NBA, shocking the sports world and her.

Last year, before the new season started, he had told her

that he never wanted to be apart from her again. That both warmed her heart and made her nervous.

She didn't want him to wake up one day and hate her because of his decision to leave the NBA—something she knew he loved. He had assured her that it was time, and he felt like it was perfect timing since he could leave on a high note after winning the finals.

After the announcement, Hunter traveled back and forth between Las Vegas and Los Angeles for months, tying up loose ends of his life. A month ago, he had finally moved to Las Vegas for good.

As for Chandra, Viviana hadn't seen or spoken to her since the day at the warehouse, and she was fine with that.

Actually, it was for the best. Malik was keeping track of Chandra, making sure she was upholding some type of agreement that she'd made with him and Quinn. Apparently, she was. She was married and living in Europe, of all places.

Viviana and Hunter reached the front door of their new home, and she thought she would explode with excitement.

"You ready?" he asked, smiling down at her.

Every time she looked into his dark eyes; her heart turned over in her chest. He made her so happy, and she loved him more than life itself.

"I'm more than ready," she said.

"Well, let's do this." Before she could say anything else, he swept her up into his arms and pushed open the door. "Welcome home, baby!"

"Surprise!"

Viviana startled and clung to Hunter's neck before she saw their family and extended family in the large foyer.

"What in the world?" she said, looking from them and back to Hunter. "What's going on?"

He set her on her feet. "I wanted them to be a part of this new chapter in our lives," he said and got down on one knee.

Viviana thought she was going to faint and grabbed on to a nearby table as tears filled her eyes. They'd talked about marriage, but she hadn't been ready when Hunter first mentioned it shortly after he had retired. But she knew she loved him, and he loved her.

"We have been through hell and back, but we've made it," he said as he held up a blue velvet box. "I thought I had lost you for good, but when you came back into my life, I knew I would never let you go again. Baby, I adore you, and I love you more than I ever thought I could love another human being. Will you do me the honor of becoming my wife...today?"

Viviana frowned when she realized what he said.

Today?

A minister stepped from the crowd of people in the hallway and was holding a little black book.

"*Today?*" she croaked, and looked at Hunter who was still on his knees.

"Yes, today. I want us to start our next chapter today as husband and wife."

A slow smile spread across her face and Viviana screamed, "Yes! Of course, I'll marry you, and I can't wait to finally be your wife!"

Everyone cheered and laughed.

Hunter opened the ring box, and Viviana froze.

"My ring," she whispered, and looked from it to Hunter. "You kept it?"

"I had to. It was my only connection I had to you, and I couldn't let it go."

Tears spilled down Viviana's face, and she fell into his arms. "Oh, my God. I can't believe you kept it. Thank you... thank you!"

She planted kisses all over his face. Besides leaving him that day, taking off that ring, a symbol of his love for her, had been one of the hardest things she'd ever done.

"You have no idea what this means to me," she said through her tears.

"I think I do," he said, wiping her face with his thumb. "This was a symbol of my love back then, and it means even more today. I love you, baby."

Though she was choked up, Viviana managed to say, "I love you, too, and I always will."

***

If you enjoyed this book, consider leaving a review on retailer's sites, review sites or social media outlets.

More Books in Series

T hank you for reading CASINO HEAT! I hope you enjoyed Hunter and Viviana's story.

If you're new to the Reunited Series, be sure to check out the rest of the stories starting with BLUE ROSES.

And if you enjoy romantic suspense, you'll love the Atlanta's Finest Series starting with A PASSIONATE KISS!

Join Sharon's Mailing List

To get sneak peeks of upcoming stories and to hear about
giveaways that Sharon is sponsoring, visit
https://sharoncooper.net/newsletter
to join her mailing list.

Other Titles By Sharon

Atlanta's Finest Series

Jenkins Family Series (Contemporary Romance)
Best Woman for the Job (Short Story Prequel)
Still the Best Woman for the Job (book 1)
All You'll Ever Need (book 2)
Tempting the Artist (book 3)
Negotiating for Love (book 4)
Seducing the Boss Lady (book 5)
Love at Last (Holiday Novella)
When Love Calls (Novella)
More Than Love (Novella)

Reunited Series (Romantic Suspense)
Blue Roses (book 1)
Secret Rendezvous (Prequel to Rendezvous with Danger)
Rendezvous with Danger (book 2)
Truth or Consequences (book 3)
Operation Midnight (book 4)
Casino Heat (book 5)

Stand Alones
Something New ("Edgy" Sweet Romance)
Legal Seduction (Harlequin Kimani – Contemporary
Romance)
Sin City Temptation (Harlequin Kimani – Contemporary
Romance)
A Dose of Passion (Harlequin Kimani – Contemporary
Romance)
Model Attraction (Harlequin Kimani – Contemporary
Romance)
Soul's Desire (Unparalleled Love series)
Show Me (Irresistible Husband series)
His to Protect (Harlequin Romantic Suspense)

Sharon C. Cooper

His to Defend (Harlequin Romantic Suspense)
Business Not As Usual (Romantic Comedy)
In It to Win It (Romantic Comedy)

About the Author

USA Today bestselling author Sharon C. Cooper loves anything involving romance with a happily-ever-after, whether in books, movies, or real life. She writes contemporary romance, as well as romantic suspense and enjoys rainy days, carpet picnics, and peanut butter and jelly sandwiches. Her stories have won numerous awards over the years, and when Sharon isn't writing, she's hanging out with her amazing husband, doing volunteer work, or reading a good book (a romance of course). To read more about Sharon and her novels, visit www.sharoncooper.net